As he stood in the ring,
a man courageous and defeated,
Rocky Balboa won the hearts of America.

Now, in ROCKY II,
he climbs back into the ring.
And this time
he will not be fighting
for money or glory—
fighting to prove he wasn't
just another bum from the block.
This time
he will be fighting for love,
for a woman,
for their child.

ROCKY II
The story continues . . .

A ROBERT CHARTOFF-IRWIN WINKLER PRODUCTION

SYLVESTER STALLONE "ROCKY II"   TALIA SHIRE   BURT YOUNG

CARL WEATHERS and BURGESS MEREDITH as MICKEY   Music by BILL CONTI

Director of Photography BILL BUTLER A.S.C.

Produced by IRWIN WINKLER and ROBERT CHARTOFF

Written and Directed by SYLVESTER STALLONE

United Artists
A Transamerica Company

ROCKY II

Sylvester Stallone

BALLANTINE BOOKS • NEW YORK

Library of Congress Catalog Card Number: 79-53552

ISBN 0-345-28650-2

Manufactured in the United States of America

First Edition: June 1979

TO YOU,
WHO LOVES TO THE END OF . . .
AN ENDLESS END.

ROCKY II

1

I REMEMBER SITTIN' on that stool thinkin' that my heart was gonna crack right outta my chest an' fall on the floor right next to the spit bucket. I ain't never been so tired, but I never felt so good either.

I just finished the fourteenth round and knew if I could hang on three more minutes, I'da done somethin' no other fighter had done—go the distance with the champion, Apollo Creed, who I was lookin' at across the ring.

Creed had been bustin' me up pretty good for the past fourteen rounds, an' every now an' then I'd get a good lick in on him; but nobody was better than Apollo Creed.

Nobody.

He stuffed that left jab into my face whenever he felt like it, an' every time he did I felt like I had lost a piece of my head. No wonder he's the best. But lucky for me he made one mistake. In the middle of the fourteenth round, he come out bombin' me with 'bout six straight right hands, a coupla choice hooks, an' another straight hand. Before I knew it I was spinnin'. Dancin' and spinnin'. But I wasn't hearin' no music. The only sound I heard was when my body bounced off the ropes an' fell into a wet spot about two feet from my corner.

This was it.

I was gonna be knocked out.

This is when all of them guys out there with their pencils, poundin' them typewriters, start writin' the word "bum" or "lucky," or "I knew he couldn't do it."

It was the quietest time of my life.

I didn't hear nobody yellin', I didn't hear no birds tweetin' inside my head, I didn't hear Mickey screamin'. I just looked across that wet spot, an' underneath the bottom rope I could see his mouth movin', his mouth was sayin', "Stay down."

He couldn't've been talkin' to me, because I had come here to stand up, not to stay down, and I knew if I didn't get up I was gonna hate myself for the rest of my life. As a matter of fact, that's what bothered me more than anythin'. I didn't care that people would say, "He's a nobody."

"He ain't nothin'."

"He couldn't go the distance."

"It was a lucky shot from South Philly."

That never bothered me. What bothered me was when I was gonna be alone, mebbe when I was fifty or sixty or ninety, and I'd look back an' say to myself, "Three more minutes, Rocky, three more; why couldn't you do it?"

Now I could hear the referee sayin' somethin' familiar. "Three . . . four . . . five . . . six . . ." I could see Apollo standin' in a neutral corner, his face all swollen an' his body breathin' real heavy-like.

Get up, Rock! Get up, get up, get up! This I kept sayin' to myself.

"Seven . . . eight . . . nine . . ."

It was a miracle, but there I was on my feet, standin', an' tellin' Creed, "Come on! Come on! Toe-to-toe!" And y'know, this guy done just that.

He come forward lookin' for the final knockout. I musta looked like every other bum he had seen in trouble, because Creed made the first mistake of the night. He took the whole thing too light, he figured the knockout was in the bag an' he shuffled toward me. He threw this lazy left hand an' a lazy right hand. Y'know, it looked like the whole thing was in slow motion to me, an' that's when I seen my openin'. I seen a lotta ribs just waitin' to get tagged.

My best punch was always a short left hook to the ribs, an' finally I got to throw it.

I heard a crack.

I threw a second left.

A second crack.

I threw two more lefts an' I seen somethin' that looked like thick wine come out of Creed's mouth. He was bleedin' inside, an' now it looked like we was both even again. I heard the bell ring an' before I knew it, there was 'bout six hands pullin' me backwards, flingin' me on a stool.

"Ya' hurt bad, kid, ya' eye's shut, ya can't go out there any more," Mickey said.

"Open my eye, Mick. C'mon, open my eye!"

"Ya wanta go blind?!"

"Yo, Mick, please open my eye, open it!"

Apollo Creed was breathing heavy. Every time

he filled up his big chest he winced in pain and more blood oozed out of the corner of his mouth. "You can't go out there no more, Champ, you're bleedin' inside, you're bleedin' bad!" his trainer said.

Mickey looked at my eye, or what used to be an eye; now it felt like a pool ball hangin' on my face. He turned to Al, the cut man, an' gave him a nod. Al had this little razor hidin' behind his pinkie finger, an' he run it across my face and brow. I heard this pop sound an' the cue ball over my eye went away. It didn't hurt. "Mickey, just three more minutes to go," I said.

"You ain't stopping nothing!" Apollo Creed yelled at his trainer.

"All right—but you gotta cover those ribs—you gotta cover those ribs and hold your elbow in!"

"You stop this fight and I'll kill you!" I yelled at Mickey. Was Mickey crazy? I was havin' the best time of my life! This was my life, an' he was gonna stop it for three minutes? That's only a coupla hundred seconds.

"All right, ya wanna go? Go!" Mickey yelled.

I knew the bell was gonna ring, so I got to my feet hopin' I could get the jump on Creed, but I looked across the ring an' seen Creed had the same thing in mind, because he was up, too.

Now for the first time I could hear the people out there, and they was yellin' my name, *"Rocky, Rocky, Rocky, Rocky,"* and it was like a huge echo through the arena. For a second I felt kind of embarrassed and wished the bell would ring. I got my wish.

I could see that Creed was tuckin' his right elbow and protectin' his ribs, knowin' that's the first place I'd aim for. And he was right.

He kept me off balance by circlin' wide, an' for a coupla heartbeats we just circled, starin' at each other, each wonderin', Who exactly is this guy across from me? What's he made of? 'Cause he ain't in it for the money now. I sure ain't.

I saw a little spark in Creed's eyes, but it was too late to do somethin' about it. Next thing I knew, a perfect right hand had caught me flush on the jaw, an' I felt my mouthpiece leave my mouth an' go sailin' out of the ring. That got me mad.

I knew now that Creed would be comin' with everythin' he had, an' everythin' he had was straight jabs, 'cause that mouthpiece punch was the last good shot he had with his right hand. I could see his ribs must've been hurtin' bad. I ducked my head an' come at him with everythin' I had. I threw a left hook to the body, a right hook to the body, another left hook to the body, an' for every two hooks I threw, Creed threw two jabs. It was like a dance. You punch, I punch, you punch twice, I punch twice.

Creed's jabs didn't bother me no more 'cause my face had been numb since the fifth round, but I could see my body punches was startin' to go through him. I could see it in his eyes. I kept thinkin', There's only a few seconds left and I'll have a shot at goin' the distance.

Another right hook.

Creed went back against the ropes! I couldn't

believe it! The champion was lyin' heavy on the top rope an' I drove a straight left into his heart which doubled him over. His hands were just hangin' there. I couldn't believe it! I could hear the audience countin' down the seconds, "Five . . . four . . . three . . ." an' that's when I wound up an' give him everythin' I had an' threw this loopin' left that landed on the chin. Creed's legs buckled!

The bell rang and the champ was goin' down, but before his knee touched, he grabbed hold of me and pulled himself upright.

"Ain't gonna be no rematch," Apollo said to me. "Don't want one."

Our corner men rushed across the ring an' pulled us apart, an' I didn't know where I was.

This was it! I had gone the distance! I had just resigned from the bum club! And the first one I wanted to tell was Adrian. Where was Adrian? I was lookin' around for her red hat movin' through the crowd, but I couldn't see nothin'. All I could see was these here flashes in my face an' microphones chargin' my mouth an' a lotta people pattin' my back. All I kept thinkin' was, Where's Adrian an' her red hat? I gotta tell her I went the distance.

"Rocky, Rocky, will there be a rematch?" a reporter asked.

"Adrian!!!" I yelled.

Where was Adrian? I was lookin' all over for her. I never wanted to talk to somebody so bad as I wanted to talk to Adrian.

The ring announcer, Miles Jergens, pushed his way through the crowd, almost knockin' one reporter over, and waved for the microphone to come down into his hand, which it done.

"Attention, please! Ladies and gentlemen, tonight

we have had the rare privilege of witnessing the greatest exhibition of guts and stamina in the history of the ring!"

Adrian was forging a path through the crowd. For a little girl she was strong, the way people were being pushed mercilessly aside. When she hit the steps leading up to the ring, a cop tried to stop her, but she avoided him and slipped between the ropes.

"Ladies and gentlemen, we have a split decision!" Miles Jergens yelled.

Apollo Creed did not expect this and he tensed up. He shook his head in disgust, and his corner man patted his shoulder and tried to reassure him that everything was going to be all right, but it did no good. A split decision meant the championship for the next thirty seconds was up for grabs.

"How'd you feel going into the last round?" a reporter with a machine-gun voice yelled at me.

I didn't want to know from this. All I wanted to know from was Adrian. "Adrian!" I yelled, "C'mon, you guys, get outta my face! I had enough things in my face tonight!"

Miles Jergens looked at the three cards in his hands and leaned closer to the microphone.

"Judge Walker scores it eight-seven, Creed! Judge Roseman scores it eight-seven, Balboa!"

I felt like I was gonna cry. Not because I might lose the fight. That didn't matter no more. I wanted to find Adrian more than I wanted to find anythin' in this world. The one night I wanted to be with her, an' she was bein' eaten up by all this confusion.

"Adrian! Adrian!"

"Rocky!" Adrian said, and stopped about two feet in front of me and looked very shy. Again I didn't hear nothin' except her breathin'. "Where's ya' red hat?" I asked.

". . . I love you!" she said and jumped up into my arms, and I held her like I never held nothin' before. And for the first time I heard some new words comin' from my stomach that I had never said to nobody before in my whole life an' I never thought I would, but now I was gonna, because I meant it. ". . . I love you, too."

Miles Jergens looked at the last card, smiled, and said, "Winner and still heavyweight champion, Apollo Creed."

2

I REMEMBER LYIN' down and hearin' this sound, it was kinda like the sound of a gnat in my ear. Then this gnat sound got louder, and then I remembered where I heard it before. I heard it before in the back of a paddy wagon when I'd been taken downtown a coupla times for doin' somethin' bad.

Well, I never did nothin' that bad. I mean, I never beat nobody up or killed nobody or stole nothin'. Y'know, I don't like people that steal. I don't like thieves, but I hate liars. At least you can watch a thief.

Yeah, I think the only time I was ever arrested was for loiterin', after some of my fights which I lost. Sometimes I'd have to hitchhike back from Paramus or Union City, New Jersey, and some rookie cop lookin' to shine his badge up in front of the sergeant would pick me up an' put me in the back of the wagon like he'd made a big score.

The ambulance siren stopped and I was kinda glad, 'cause I was gettin' a headache. And I looked up an' there was Adrian sittin' on some small metal

9

thing next to the cot. She smiled and ran them light fingers of hers along my arm, which made my arm feel very good at that moment.

I heard a voice an' then the back door of the ambulance swung open, and before I knew it I was whipped out of there and put into a wheelchair. I'd just stood fifteen rounds with the champion of the world, so I think I could've stood with a coupla interns an' nurses, but they didn't want to hear 'bout that. I was put in the wheelchair an' they wheeled me through the doors.

I seen a few photographers standin' along the side there, snappin' bulbs and askin' questions, but my jaw was too sore to talk, so I just kinda waved.

From out of nowhere Mickey come alongside, an' with him was Pauline, an' I felt very good in general havin' my friends around at a time like this. It weren't no victory party, but then again, it weren't no funeral either.

"Give 'im some air!" Paulie yelled, and pushed somebody out of the way.

I rolled past a coupla Puerto Rican kids an' their mother waitin' for some kinda emergency treatment, an' they waved at me until they got a good look at my face. I could see they were— what's the word I'm lookin' for?—yeah, "horrified." They was horrified. I don't know what they was horrified about. I'm the one who had to live with it, and it didn't bother me none.

"It's Rocky Balboa!" Paulie yelled to everybody.

"Whod'they think it is?" Mickey said just low enough so I could hear him. I don't think Mickey and Paulie was ever gonna be friends. They just weren't the same kind of street guys.

"Way to do it, man! Shake my hand, my man," a Puerto Rican guy said an' tried to grab my hand.

Paulie grabbed him hard by the wrist, this I could see out of the corner of my good eye, an' flung him outta the way. "No hands! No handshakin' here! You don't see no sign sayin' shake Rocky's hand, do ya?!" Paulie yelled and kept me rollin'.

Adrian was standin' on my left, so I had a hard time seein' her. As a matter of fact, I couldn't see her at all, but I could feel her touchin' my shoulder an' I could almost hear her breathin'. I knew she was there and it made me feel very good.

I knew this was the high point of my life. I knew that every minute after this was downhill. I knew it was gonna be an impossible act to follow, because I had tied all my dreams up in one shot.

I had gone the distance with the champ, I had proved myself to the people, I had proved myself to me, an' I had said "I love you" for the first time. Yeah, I'd make odds that this was gonna be the best night of my life.

I seen a lot of photographers and reporters comin' through another door an' they all were shovin' and pushin' each other to get good picture-takin' positions.

"The doctor will be right here, Rocky," Adrian said and looked around.

"Where's the doctor?" asked Mickey.

"He'll be taken into the emergency room in a moment," a young intern answered. "Would you like to fill out these insurance forms in the mean-time?"

Paulie bumped right into him, took the insurance forms out of his hand, and said, "This I'll do."

Let's see—I'd estimate there was now twenty reporters and ten photographers standin' in front of me just snappin' pictures, askin' questions, an' makin' jokes between themselves. I seen Paulie kind of slide behind me an' put his face next to mine and smile at the photographers. Y'know, in sixteen, seventeen years I know this guy, he ain't never changed.

"Paulie!" Adrian yelled.

"What's wrong with publicity? Do ya mind, Rock?" Paulie said and stuck out his chin like his feelin's had been hurt. I shook my head "no" and Paulie made an I-told-you-so face at his sister an' went back to fillin' out them papers he had in his hand.

I turned to Adrian and said, "Paulie's all right, he ain't doin' no damage." Then I turned to Mickey and said, "How bad's my nose? Bad as yours?"

"Naw . . . couple whacks with a hammer'll fix everythin'," Mickey said.

A couple more flashes went off in my face an' I heard a squeaky voice comin' out from behind a pad and pencil.

"Is this the most punishment you've ever taken?" a skinny reporter asked.

Paulie took a step toward him. "You're gonna get worse if you don't get outta here!"

"Will there be a rematch?" another reporter asked.

"No rematch! That's all!" Mickey said and turned his back on the group.

I touched Mickey's sleeve and he leaned down. "What time is it?" I said.

Mickey checked his watch. "Twelve-ten. Why?"

". . . just curious." I really just wanted to know what time it was, but I seen Mickey and Adrian exchange worried looks and then Adrian started to look around the room for a doctor. She probably thought I was sinkin' fast. I wasn't goin' punchy.

"Where's the doctor?" Adrian said, louder than she'd said anythin' all night, except for the time she said, "I love you."

"Where's the damn doctor?!" Mickey yelled.

A reporter came right up behind Mickey and tapped him on the shoulder. "Will the doctor perform surgery tonight?"

Mickey grabbed him by the collar and got his mouth about an inch away from the reporter's nose and yelled, "On *you* if ya don't get away from us, ya screwy bastards!"

More and more flashes went off in my face, and I could see why King Kong went nuts on that stage when them reporters was doin' the same thing to him. Mickey was about to take a swing at one of them guys when the door at the other end of the hall swung open an' I seen all these people rush through.

Then I seen Apollo Creed in a wheelchair just like mine. He was still a popular guy. There must've been fifty people followin' behind him, yellin' good things and tryin' to pat his wheelchair or anythin' to get close to the guy.

"Recognize that guy?" Mickey said.

Apollo motioned for one of his people to roll him toward me, and he yelled, "Stallion!"

"That's a familiar face I hear," I said and tried to smile.

Creed pulled right up next to me an' we were lookin' at each other, an' if I looked as bad as he looked, I was hopin' somebody would take me into the woods somewheres and leave me. Both of us looked like we tried to kiss an RTD bus goin' at eighty miles an hour.

"The Italian Stallion! You got a dull skull, Stallion! You're the luckiest man alive!" the champion yelled.

"Do I look lucky, Apollo?"

"You don't go the distance with me—I'll fight you any place, any time!"

I couldn't believe he was so mad. "Yo, ya serious?"

"Get outta that chair and you'll see who's serious!"

A reporter stepped up to Apollo. "Apollo, were you going down? Did the bell save you?"

"Bell nothin'. I'll fight him any place, any time."

"Does that mean there's going to be a rematch?"

"Any place—any time!"

"Yo, Apollo, ya said there weren't gonna be no rematch!"

"Any place—any time!"

"I'm retired."

"Hey, you don't back down on me! I gave you a shot, now I'm givin' you a second shot!"

I turned to Adrian. "He sure has a lotta energy."

Mickey pointed at the reporters. "Listen, I don't care what them judges say—I say Rocky won!"

"You punched his lungs out—we think you're the champ!" Paulie said, loud enough for the dead to hear.

". . . thank you," I said.

"You're gonna fight me again! Then you gonna see how lucky you were—you gonna fight me!" Apollo yelled as he was being rolled away.

Adrian come over and touched my shoulder. "They're ready, Rocky."

I touched her hand an' said, "Mebbe you'd better go home. I think I'm gonna be busy healin' for a while." I didn't really want her to go. I never wanted her to go nowhere. I'd like to have an Adrian around until the day I croak.

"Do you really want me to go?"

"Mebbe you better."

"I'll be here," Adrian said.

I was in the middle of a sore smile when one of them young guys in a white coat with ink stains over the chest pockets come up and pushed me around the corner.

"I'll be here," Adrian called after me.

3

I DIDN'T KNOW what that smell was. I mean, I did know what the smell was, but I didn't know what I was doin' in the middle of that smell. I mean, it was that knockout smell, the gas or the ether, or whatever these here hospitals use to knock you out with. But the smell didn't seem right tonight, because just an hour ago I was feelin' better than I'd ever felt in my life.

I proved I weren't no bum from the neighborhood, I should be celebratin', but instead I was bein' covered by hospital smells. I never liked emergency rooms, even if it was an emergency.

About three interns were busy tryin' to clean me up and stickin' somethin' they called, I forgot the name, but boy, these doctors were definitely goin' for the knockout, 'cause I could feel the room spinnin', and spinnin', and spinnin'.

"I gotta ask a question," I said, and my voice sounded like I was in the bottom of a dented trash can.

"Yes?" one of the guys in white coats answered.

"Is my face gonna look like liver?"

"You'll look just fine. Please, try to relax."

"I'm very relaxed. Can ya fix my nose? . . . I'm depressed about the nose."

"We'll set that, too."

"Y'know, I ain't never felt this great . . . I really . . . feel . . . great."

4

PAULIE AND ADRIAN left the hospital and walked slowly through the glass doors down the steps toward the cab stand.

"The Rock was great tonight, wasn't he?" Paulie said.

". . . yes."

"It reminded me of the fight I had with that guy who called ya ugly—I never told ya about that guy. He said ya was a very ugly person an' I broke all his teeth. 'Course I never told ya about that."

"Thank you, Paulie," Adrian said.

"Ya gonna marry him?"

"Yes."

"I had a feelin' ya were gonna do that."

"Don't you think that's good, Paulie?"

"Good?"

"Yes, good."

"Adrian, c'mere, I wanna talk honest with ya. I know the Rock—what—fifteen, sixteen years? An' him I just wouldn't expect to change."

"I think we'll manage, Paulie."

"Sure ya will, ya always had a smart head—but ya an' him ain't got the same kinda attic." Paulie tapped his temple. "See, once ya get a taste of the top, it's hard goin' back to what ya used to be. It's gonna be hard for me cuttin' meat again, ya know. C'mon, get in the taxi," Paulie tried to move Adrian toward the yellow car.

"You go. I'm staying here, Paulie."

Paulie was still not used to Adrian thinking for herself, and that bothered him a lot. You could tell it bothered him, because his mouth would move and nothing would come out. It was as if someone had broken the volume switch on his throat.

He pointed his finger at Adrian, then he pointed his finger at the taxi and pulled open the door.

"Get in the taxi, I says. You need ya' sleep."

"I'll be all right . . . Good night, Paulie," Adrian said and turned to walk back into the hospital.

At that moment Paulie finally realized that his sister was no longer just someone to cook the meals and clean up after the Sunday ball game in front of the television and stuff like that. His sister was now a person, and that was a big shock to Paulie.

"Good night, Adrian . . ." he said and idly touched his neck. "Yo, y'know I'd like to see ya around the house sometime, Adrian."

The door slammed shut and she watched the exhaust cloud out of the rattling taxi's tailpipe until it blended into the Philadelphia backdrop.

5

THE FIRST THING I seen when I woke up was Tony Gazzo. I don't know how Tony Gazzo ever got into the hospital; all I know is, Tony Gazzo's put a lot of guys in the hospital. But there he was sittin' beside the bed with a bunch of flowers in his right hand. Me, I felt like I was lookin' at life through a dirty windshield, 'cause the lights were low an' I had this heavy bandage over my right eye that must've weighed five pounds. These doctors sure wasted a lot of time an' bandages on my eye. I hope it was worth it.

" . . . I thought ya had him in the tenth," Tony said and twisted his pinkie ring. "Then in the fifteenth he was goin'—ya almost made the odds, kid. How's your face feel?"

"Not bad," I said. My voice sounded like it was comin' out of my nose. "How's it look?"

"I wouldn't want it," Gazzo said.

I laughed an' felt the bandage on my face an' somehow knew that I kinda resembled a mummy from South Philly. Didn't bother me too much; I hope it didn't bother nobody else lookin' at me. Then I remembered somethin'. I wanted to do somethin' for Paulie.

"Hey, Tony, could ya do me a favor?"

"What?"

"Y'know Paulie, my friend. Could ya give him my old job with ya?"

"Collectin'?"

"He's good with numbers."

"He's a slob."

"He admires ya."

". . . sure, for you, kid."

The door opened and I seen this nurse come in. It was the first time I'd seen her, but I could tell by the way she walked into this room that she'd walked into this room a lotta times, mebbe ten thousand. She was very shocked when she seen Gazzo sittin' by my bed. She walked right up to him an' acted like she weren't afraid at all.

"What are you doing here? Visiting hours are over."

"Let me explain the situation," Gazzo said and smiled. "Here's the situation, doll. Rocky Balboa's a relative of mine, first cousin, an' in any language that should mean visitin' privileges," Gazzo said in a smooth way.

The nurse wasn't shook by it at all. "You'll have to leave," she said.

"Sure, doll . . . Rocky, whatever you need, I'll be around."

I watched Tony stand up and couldn't help admirin' the way he was dressed. Even when he was poor and livin' around Front Street, just a coupla blocks from the docks, Tony always managed to steal somethin' off the back of a truck that would keep him well dressed. Some people would steal

cases of beer or Coke or light bulbs to sell; not
Tony, he always went for the garments. Shoes,
gloves, hats, and anythin' else that would make him
look like a peacock in a neighborhood of pigeons.

With my good eye I seen the nurse come forward
with a pill cup fulla stuff that makes ya feel happy
when ya' body feels bad.

"How do we feel tonight?" the nurse said.

I knew she was gonna say that. On every TV
show I'd seen for the past twenty years, the nurse
always comes into some guy's room who's got his
legs blown off or half his head gone or his ears
chewed off by a junkyard dog or somethin' like that,
and she asks the same question: "How do we feel
tonight?"

"Never better," I said. "Yo, could ya tell me the
number on the door Apollo Creed is stayin' in?"

"Which room? Number twenty-three. Now get
some sleep, Mr. Balboa."

". . . you, too."

The nurse was headin' for the door when she
stopped in them white shoes she was wearin' and
turned around toward me. "I almost forget. My son
would love your autograph. Would you sign it, 'To
my good friend, Charlie Flynn'?"

This nurse didn't almost forget nothin,' because
she had a pad and pen ready. I dislike signin' autographs in general, not that that many people have
asked me to scribble my name, but that's what I do,
I scribble. I always had bad, whaddaya call it,
penmanship, and I was always the guy that the
teacher would hold up as an example. The teacher
would say if you don't study and practice crossin' *t*'s
and dottin' your *i*'s and makin' nice *o*'s, you're gonna
end up writin' like Rocky Balboa, which is the same

as givin' a monkey a pen and turnin' him loose. I
use to think that was funny.

"Would you sign it, 'To my good friend, Charlie
Flynn'?" the nurse said again. I followed the orders
an' scribbled the worst-lookin' autograph in the history of writin' an' give it back to her. She smiled,
took her pill cup, and walked out of the room without ever makin' a sound.

I watched the door close an' got outta bed an'
walked to a small mirror. It's the first time I'd stood
up since the fight, and I gotta tell you somethin',
already I felt out of shape. When you start gettin'
up around thirty years old, there ain't no question
about it, the legs start to rot.

I looked into the mirror an' tried to figure out
what that mess was starin' back at me. I kinda felt
sick, lookin' at it, but then again, I kinda felt proud,
too, like it was a badge of honor that those Cub
Scouts or Boy Scouts would earn when they do good.
I had done pretty good and this was my merit badge.

I only wish everybody who had ever called me a
moron in my whole life could see me now. Y'know
how kids are in third, fourth, fifth, sixth grade . . .
and seventh and eighth grade, too. I don't know how
they are after that, 'cause I didn't stick around for
them.

Yeah, I wish they all could see me now, 'cause I
had been the punchline for a lotta people's jokes
for a lotta years and finally I had done good. And
for the first time in my two-bit life, I was proud of
myself.

Then I thought about the autograph I just signed:
"To my good friend, Charlie Flynn . . . who I don't
even know."

6

THE DOOR TO Apollo Creed's room squeaked a little bit as I pushed it open. And as it opened wider and wider, this thin piece of light was inchin' across the room. It almost inched its way up to Apollo's bed when I had opened the door wide enough for me to slip in out of the hallway.

I still couldn't see Creed so good, so I opened the door just a little bit more an' the light from the hall lit up Creed's face. "Apollo—Apollo?" I said in my nose voice.

"Who's that?"

"Me, Rocky. Answer me one question."

"What?"

"Did ya give me ya' best?"

"Yes," the champ said.

That's all I wanted to hear. I didn't wanna hear no more. And I made sure I was very quiet when I slipped out into the hall an' headed toward my room.

I was very tired by the time I got back there. I

don't know why. Hadn't I just gone fifteen rounds with the greatest fighter that ever laced on a pair of gloves? Now I was tired walkin' just fifty feet . . . I made sure I was quiet when I opened my bedroom door. I couldn't wait to lie down and dream about what a day it had been. As I was movin' closer to the bed, I thought I saw somethin' with my good eye in the corner of the room. A second later I was sure I did see somethin' that I'd been wantin' to see all night. Y'know, at first it looked like a shadow, but Adrian weren't no shadow. She was somethin' bright to me, somethin' light to me, she was me and I was her.

It's as simple as that.

When she moved to me very slowly, kinda like she was made outta smoke, I could see that she'd been cryin' a little bit, an' without sayin' nothin' she just put her head on my chest. An' I put my arms around her an' I knew no matter what happened, ever in my life,

I knew that I would always
love this
quiet woman.

7

I WAS WALKIN' in the hospital hallway and I was feelin' good. A few days had passed an' I was feelin' a lot better, except for this bandage over my eye. I didn't know how much longer I had to carry this thing around, but I felt very stupid walkin' around with this bird's nest on my face.

It looks like a lotta people hadn't forgotten me, 'cause as I walked down the hall I seen a lotta people noddin' an' smilin', an' I reached over an' took Adrian's arm. Touchin' her always makes me feel healthier.

There were these two guys who were pretty well dressed standin' on both sides of me. I'd say they was about thirty-five years old or somethin' like that, but they was very slick types. They said they was agents, an' I guess ya gotta be pretty slick to be an agent. One guy did most of the talkin'. "The agency can almost guarantee commercial fees in excess of $300,000 the next fiscal year."

I eyeballed the contracts that was in the agent's

hand an' couldn't help noticin' the kinda jewelry he wore.

I'd estimate they were successful.

I leaned over to the shorter one and said, "You're gonna guarantee me money just for talkin' 'bout some shavin' stuff?"

"Plus a wide variety of other products."

Now the other agent spoke up. "The point is, we have to set things in motion while your name is still in everybody's mind."

"Then ya's better hurry," I said.

"Why don't we sit down and discuss this in more detail?"

"Listen, I'll sign whatever ya want, but we got more important things to do."

"More important than this?" He looked surprised.

"Absolutely. I'll call ya."

Me and Adrian left.

8

IT WAS SNOWIN' in the zoo as me an' Adrian walked by the cages. Almost none of the animals liked the snow, so me an' Adrian had the whole zoo to ourselves . . . an' that was good, 'cause I had to ask Adrian some pretty important questions.

"How do ya feel?"

"I feel good," Adrian said.

"Do ya feel excellent, or just good?"

"I feel very good. Why?"

"Just wonderin'. But you do feel very, very good —not just a regular good, right?"

"Yes, I feel very, very, very good," Adrian said and laughed.

Y'know, all my life I knew usin' words weren't gonna be my specialty. I wanted to ask some important questions, but I couldn't figure how to slide into it. I seen the one tiger was out in the snow. It looked like he liked the weather, so we curbed our way toward his cage. The tiger looked great even if he was behind bars an' surrounded by this river thing.

"Nice, tiger," I said.

"Nice."

"Looks nice an' friendly," I said an' laughed at how borin' I was. "It's nice bein' outside. I was gettin' tired of lyin' down for three weeks."

"I'm sure."

I had to say somethin' interestin' soon or Adrian was gonna be asleep in the snow.

"How do ya feel?"

"I feel fine, Rocky."

"Well, I was wonderin' . . . like . . . y'know, I was thinkin' that—y'know—ah . . . whatta ya have planned for the next forty or fifty years?"

"What do you mean?"

"Well, I myself was, y'know . . . I was wonderin' if you would mind marryin' me too much."

"What?"

Adrian didn't hear what I was tryin' to say, 'cause I was talkin' real quiet-like and she had on these here earmuffs. I pulled back one of the earmuffs and said, "Would ya mind marryin' me too much?"

"Yes, I want to," Adrian said real fast-like.

"Ya do?!"

"Oh, yes!"

I hugged and kissed her.

"Listen, I'm gonna be a good guy, y'know—I ain't leavin' no hair in the sink or doin' bad things —yo, Adrian! Thanks!"

We kissed and kissed a lot more.

9

IT WAS OUR wedding day. We were in church and me and Adrian was standin' in front of Father Carmine. We was all dressed up real special-like, like ya' supposed to be when ya get married.

Adrian looked like some dream. She had on a long white gown and a veil around her face that made her look like an angel. She was very quiet and her hands were shaking.

". . . to be ya' lawfully wedded wife?" Father Carmine said.

"Absolutely, yes," I smiled at Adrian.

"Then you may kiss the bride."

I pulled back that veil that was covering Adrian's face and I kissed her real good-like. "It's gonna be great," I said to Adrian. Then, to Father Carmine, "Thanks, Father, ya done real good." Paulie and Gazzo come right up and slapped me on the back.

"Good luck, ya' gonna need it," Paulie said.

"Good move, Rock—it was pretty nice," Gazzo said.

Gloria, the owner of the Pet Shop, where Adrian used to work, was sittin' next to Mickey, who was havin' a hard time stayin' awake. Gloria come up to me.

"Good luck to you."

"Thank you, Gloria," Adrian said and held my arm tighter.

"Yeah, congratulations. Hey, Rock, ya wanna buy into the pet store? It's a solid place."

"Thanks, Gloria, but I'm gonna do commercials."

"Commercials for what? Bruises?"

"Yeah, bruises," I said and looked at Mickey. "How ya doin', Mick?"

"Fine. Listen, good luck to ya both—I gotta get back to the gym. I got some good prospects."

"Yeah, they good?"

"Yeah. I'll see ya, kid."

I watched Mickey turn an' head outta the church. Good guy, old Mick.

Paulie pinched my cheek. "C'mon, let's get drunk!"

Gazzo come up next to me. "Wait, Paulie, I wanna talk to the bridegroom here—c'mere, Rock." Gazzo turned to Adrian and winked. "Ya look beautiful, kid. Over here, Rock." I followed Gazzo off to the side of the altar.

"This weddin' was nice . . . so let's hear it— what'd ya clear on the fight?"

"'Bout thirty-seven grand," I said, wanting to get back to Adrian bad.

"Taxes kill ya. So whatta ya wanna do? Want me to put some bread on the street for ya? Let it work for ya?"

I was really embarrassed. "Hey, Tony, I just got married in this church."

"An' I'm happy for ya. Maybe ya should put ten grand on the street—I'll double ya money."

"Thanks, but we got plans—me an' Adrian."

"Ha, it's good ya got plans. How 'bout investin' in condominiums?"

I must have turned really red 'cause I was feelin' my face get very hot. I couldn't believe Tony was talkin' about condominiums in church!

". . . did you say condominiums?"

"Yeah, condominiums!"

". . . I never use them."

10

AFTER GETTIN' MARRIED, we all went over to Andy's bar an' done some serious drinkin'. Most everybody was happy an' a lotta people asked for autographs. Paulie was askin' me to let him handle Adrian if she gave me any trouble—he'd be happy to knock her teeth out, he said. I think Paulie is a little crazy. I hope Gazzo can handle him now that he's Gazzo's collector.

Well, I was startin' to feel really romantic, ya know, an' wanted to get outta Andy's now. I could see Adrian was feelin' the same way. So I stood up an' said, "The drinks is on me an' Adrian tonight!" Me an' Adrian shook a lotta hands as we was movin' to the door. We finally got out an' the last thing I heard was, "Here's to Rocky, who's a good guy no matter what nobody says."

11

IT MUSTA RAINED when we was in Andy's joint, 'cause the street was all wet. I was cold, too. God, I knew every crack in the street that led back to my old apartment. When I wasn't workin' or fightin' or doin' anythin' worth a darn, I would always find new things to do in the street. Like, first I would count the lines in the cement, but that was no big deal, anybody could do that. Then I would measure off how many footsteps there was from the corner to my door. Sometimes when I really had nothin' to do, I would try to add up all the house numbers on my block in my head and come up with the answer by the time I got to my place.

That I could never do.

I picked Adrian up and walked down the street carryin' her in my arms 'cause I was still feelin' very romantic. Bein' all dressed the way we was, people thought we were escaped nuts.

"How do you feel about all of this?" Adrian said.

" 'Bout what?"

"About bein' married."

"Very good in general."

"Think it's changing you?"

"No, I feel very normal an' nothin's wrong with changin', Adrian, long as we're changin' for the good . . . Y'know, Adrian, he was goin' down in the last round, Creed was, y'know?"

"I thought you retired?"

She was right. I had gone an' retired an' that was that. I had given her my word an' I was out of the fight game; besides, I was loaded, I was a walkin' bank. I held her closer. She was like a key. I was a lock an' she was the key. I hugged her an' I kissed her an' for a split second I thought of Apollo Creed.

He was goin' down in the last round.

We come under the Railroad Bridge on Kensington Avenue an' swung up my street. Right away this good music come into my ears—Adrian's ears, too, since she was still in my arms. Yeah, my arms was about to fall off, but I weren't gonna admit that—it might embarrass her.

Right near the corner was this here small alley. The only thing it was ever used for was throwin' ya' empty beer or wine bottle into when ya was done. An' sometimes it was used for singin' 'cause it had this really good echo, y'know. I could see Adrian was a little nervous when we peeled into the alley. Then she really got nervous when she seen five guys standin' around a burnin' trash can singin' an' tippin' wine. They stopped singin' an' tried for a coupla seconds to focus their eyes.

"Hey, Rock, how ya doin'?"

"Good, real good. This is Adrian."

"What happened, man?"

"We got married. This is Adrian!"

"All right!"

"Way to do it, man."

"Say hi, Adrian."

"Hi."

"All right. How 'bout you an' ya' ol' lady have some wine?"

"Thanks, but we got some things to do. See ya's later."

Me an' Adrian moved on up the middle of the street. Boy, nobody was awake except them singers, an' their music really sounded good on these empty streets.

"Who are they?"

"Them, they're like the neighborhood's jukebox, singin' all the time . . . I never knew you was so light!"

"Never?"

"No, if I did, I woulda carried ya everywhere."

"Do you remember the first time we walked up this street?"

"Absolutely. November twenty-seventh—ah, 'bout ten-thirty in the evenin'. I even remember the temperature."

"No, you don't, do you?"

"Sure. It started out very cold, an' by the end of the night I was burnin' up!"

Adrian laughed. I loved to hear her laugh, it made me laugh.

"Aren't you gettin' tired, Rocky?"

"Nah, this carryin' is great for the arms—I think it is . . . "

"I can't believe we're really married."

"Yo, we are, I got proof in my pocket!"

"It all happened so quick, didn't it?"

"Yeah, but I knew what was gonna happen from the start."

"What did you know?"

I put my foot on the first step of the boarding house's steps an' hoped I wouldn't trip. "Well, I said the first time I seen ya, I says to myself, I said this is the girl I want to marry. She's special, an' even though she has the disease of bein' shy, underneath that hat, glasses, an' what'd ya have on, 'bout twenty sweaters?"

"Three," Adrian laughed.

"Under them three sweaters is the best girl in Philly."

"Did you really?"

"Oh, yeah—yes, I did!"

We was gettin' closer to my room, an' I couldn't wait, 'cause my arms was ready to explode.

"Yeah, it was definitely big love at first sight."

"But I was so afraid."

"That didn't bother me none. I got a lotta patience, Adrian. If ya didn't like me, I was willin' to hang around for a long time."

"How long?" Adrian laughed again.

"I was willin' to wait for ya up to forty years, but after that I woulda had to make other plans, y'know."

Adrian smiled and kissed me. "How are your arms now?"

"Gettin' longer . . . Ya got the key?"

I was still holdin' Adrian an' she unlocked the door. When the door opened, I seen Butkus, our dog, was sleepin' on our bed.

"Here we are, safe an' sound . . . Yo, Butkus, could ya find another seat, please."

Butkus yawned an' moved slower than anythin' I ever seen move slow, to his bed in the corner. I stared into Adrian's eyes. "You're beautiful."

"Really think so?"

"You're the best thing that ever come into my crazy life," I said an' carried her to the bed. I was real careful the way I put her down, then I sat next to her. Her brown hair layin' on that pillow was the prettiest thing I ever seen.

"Do you think it will always be like this?" Adrian almost whispered.

"Oh, yeah."

"I hope you never get—"

"What?"

"Tired of me."

"Ya' never gettin' rid of me."

I felt myself gettin' closer to her, like I was bein' pulled real soft-like toward her lips.

"I hope nothing ever changes," she said.

My voice was almost gone. Everythin' I ever wanted was in front of my eyes.

"I'm not changin' . . . an' I'm sure not ever changin' nothin' about you . . ."

12

APOLLO CREED WAS lying in bed with his wife. She was asleep, but the champ wasn't. Apollo was restless, and after trying two or three different positions in order to get back to sleep, he finally gave up, got up, and went into the bathroom.

He stood in the dark for the longest time before he reached up and flicked the light switch. He was slow in the way he moved toward the sink, and he was hard in the way he stared at the picture of Rocky taped on the mirror. He took a deep breath and continued to stare. Then, absently, he moved over and sat on the edge of the tub and rested his face in his hands.

13

THIS I HAD a hard time believin', but here I was, me, Rocky Balboa, part-time bum, standin' in City Hall. Standin' in a room full of the shiniest, best-lookin' wood I ever seen. Standin' a few feet away from His Honor himself, the Mayor. This was the craziest thing I'd ever heard of. Yeah, here I was lookin' around, an' all I seen were the highest ceilings I'd ever seen. I don't know why they wasted so much room, 'cause you coulda put another floor up there, there musta been twenty-five feet. Either they wasted a lot of space buildin', or I guess they were plannin' ahead in case they ever elected a very, very, very tall mayor.

What a dumb joke.

It was hard for me to take my eyes off the Mayor. First of all, he was a lot bigger than I seen in the newspapers. He'd make a pretty good heavyweight. His shiny black hair was really lit up this afternoon, because a few feet away were a couple of them minicameras, I think they're called, filming all this stuff down so it could be flashed on the news tonight.

And right behind them cameramen were about twenty or twenty-six reporters, somethin' like that, and behind them were about fifty people, nobody I'd ever known in this life, that's for sure. I guess they were just people who wandered in to catch the show.

"Rocky Balboa," the Mayor said, "the great city of Philadelphia is honored to bestow on one of its favorite sons this plaque to serve as a reminder of one of the finest moments in sports, and as a symbol of pride for every Philadelphian for years to come."

I gotta admit, the last part of that speech got me a little choked inside, y'know. It made my stupid stomach go into kinda a knot. I was the luckiest pug in the whole world, 'cause here I was, having important people say important things about me in a very important place, which is what City Hall is. The last time I felt this emotional over somethin' was the time I seen Secretariat race in the Kentucky Derby. I was down at Andy's bar an' I was watchin' this thing on television. Secretariat was a champ, all right, but nobody knew how much of a champ.

Instead of goin' out as a winner, he went out as a legend. He didn't just win that race, he demolished everybody. After a coupla minutes Secretariat was racin' against himself, nobody else. An' that's the kind of feelin's I was havin'. I'd always been racin' against me an' nobody else. Then I looked over at Adrian. She was prettier than I'd ever seen her, an' standin' back there against them shiny wood walls, I thought she looked like one of them queens from England. I was more proud for her than I was for myself, y'know. It must've been a heck of a gamble for her to get tied up with me an' I guess it paid off, because we'd really done somethin' good together. I figured I'd better get up an' talk to the Mayor, since it was the second time they asked me, so I walked forward and we shook hands and the Mayor handed me this plaque and it was pretty heavy. "This is pretty heavy," I said. "Thank you, Mr. Mayor. I'll try to do good by this."

"I'm sure you will," the Mayor said.

"Rocky, now that you've retired, what kind of work will you seek?" a reporter asked.

"Somethin' easy, y'know."

"Like what?" another reporter asked.

"Run for mayor," I said.

I was hopin' that the Mayor would laugh an' he did, then he raised his dukes and squared off with me and put his fist on my chin and my fist on his chin, and all them cameras just popped away.

I was really proud Adrian could see this.

14

HERE I WAS in a place I'd never been before. I was sittin' in this high chair, the kind they use in beauty shops or places like that. A skinny guy with a lot of gold chains hangin' around his neck was puttin' this makeup on my face, tryin' to make me look pretty. If any of the guys on the corner had seen this, they probably would have drug me in an alley and smacked me around and thought I was turnin' into some kinda fruitcake. But luckily, it was just me and this guy with the gold chains hangin' around, and, of course, Adrian. Adrian was always there.

She smiled at me as the makeup man put some powder on my face, and he said, "Are you nervous?"

"Me?" I said. "No, I ain't nervous . . . Yo, you got any deodorant in your bag?"

I was standin' in this place they call the wings and lookin' out at all them bright lights an' this famous guy named Mike Douglas. A lot of times when I wasn't workin' for Gazzo, I'd hang around

Andy's bar an' watch Mike Douglas in the afternoon. Adrian was holdin' my sweaty hand and standin' behind me and pattin' me on the shoulder about every four or five seconds. Them two agents, they just kept smilin' and sayin' things like, "You're gonna be a smash!"

Mike Douglas, he walked out into the middle of the stage, and all the lights went on and the sign that said "Applause" started flashin' and like magic everybody started clappin'. I was shocked. I guess the audience is nervous, too, 'cause if they need a sign to remind them how to clap their hands together, they must be feelin' as shaky as I do right now. Again the agent tapped my shoulder, and I wanted to tell him to save it till I needed it, but I didn't want to hurt the little guy's feelings. I leaned over to Adrian and whispered in her ear, "Did you eat lunch?"

"Yes."

"That's good," I said and looked up at this little television they had backstage.

There I was lookin' at Mike Douglas on stage with my real eyes, and then I could see him on a small television set a few feet above my head. It was kinda interesting, it was like bein' farsighted and nearsighted at the same time.

Adrian squeezed my hand and said, "Are you nervous?"

"My body's sweatin' a little," I said and felt another drop run down from underneath my arm almost to my belt.

The audience was laughin' at a lot of things that Mike was sayin', and then he got around to talkin' about me. "Today we have a favorite son from Philadelphia—a man who many call a million-to-one shot . . ."

I turned to Adrian and whispered, "Is he talkin' about me?"

"I think so." Adrian smiled. The shorter of the two agents—the reason I say shorter is 'cause I still didn't even know their names; so when I would talk to Adrian about these two agents, I would call one short and the other one shorter. Shorter said, "Now we can start a public saturation campaign," and winked.

". . . a two-fisted southpaw from South Philly—let's all welcome the Italian Stallion, Rocky Balboa!" Mike said.

I was more scared now than I ever was with Apollo. With Apollo I knew he was gonna try to bust my face up, but with this guy Mike Douglas I had no idea what was gonna happen. I wanted to move, but my legs had grown roots an' they was stickin' to the floor. I looked at Adrian an' she knew what I was thinkin' an' she squeezed my hand a little tighter and said, "These people want to see you, they like you, there's nothing to be nervous about."

"That's easy for you to say, you stay back here," I said and smiled a little. Ah, what the heck, might as well go meet Mike. I walked down to the stage, an' the band played some sort of snappy tune that I didn't know the name of, an' there I was in front of all these strangers an' lights an' cameras an' Mr. Mike Douglas himself. I felt my knees startin' into rice puddin' an' I felt like I might fold like an accordion any second.

"Welcome, Rocky," Mike Douglas said.

"What . . . do I do?"

"What would you like to do, Rocky?"

"How 'bout some pushups?" I said.

The audience laughed a little, and I figured I'd

done pretty good and looked over at the agents standin' with Adrian off stage there. They weren't laughin'. One agent was shakin' his head an' rubbin' his eyes, and the shorter guy just shrugged his shoulders.

Some people
are
very hard to please,
you know.

15

Now I was on another show that I ain't never heard of before. It was a show that comes on late at night. Usually I flop out around eleven o'clock, so I never seen this show before. It was called the *Tomorrow Show* and it weren't no show that was built for laughs, like the *Mike Douglas Show* were. This here guy, Tom Snyder, who was the boss, kinda reminded me of a lot of the smarter people I had met in my life. He talked smart, he looked smart, so I figured mathematically he must be smart. There weren't no audience around when I was there, just the guys that work there, an' it was very dark, too. I sat in this little chair and he sat in his chair smokin' a cigarette, and I had a feeling he was gonna keep askin' me serious questions all night long.

"Rocky, don't you believe that you represent a resurgence in the American dream?"

I knew it. "Yeah, I believe in America," I said.

"And that everybody has a chance of fulfilling his dream?" he said, and took a deep, important drag on his cigarette.

"Absolutely."

"Yet I think statistics show that this country does not provide that many opportunities for people's dreams, and your 'going the distance' is the exception to the rule, is it not?"

"Maybe, but Mickey, my trainer, used to say, 'If ya face life with the eye of the alley cat, you never get lost in the city.' "

Now, I figured I said somethin' pretty smart, even though I'd said it twenty times before in a lot of different places, but I figured it was pretty smart, especially comin' from me. Then Tom Snyder crossed his legs the other way, leaned forward, looked deep into my face, and asked, "Rocky, are you punchy?"

"No—I got a relaxed brain."

I guess he bought that, 'cause he turned to the camera, flicked his ash, and said to the little red light, "We'll be right back with our show, 'What Is a Rocky Balboa?' "

After the *Tomorrow Show,* I took a trip out to Los Angeles and met with a group of guys I've been wantin' to meet with for a long time. These guys were ex-pugs, and they had gotten together and started a club called the Cauliflower Alley Club. And I thought that was pretty nice, because there wasn't a place for boxers to go when they got finished with their craft. Most of them ended up as doormen or taxi drivers or down on Skid Row talkin' about all the bad decisions they had gotten. These guys here would meet once a week an' talk about the good old days, an' I thought that was nice, yeah, I thought that was real nice.

So here I was with all them great fighters from the old days. They seated me behind a long table with a lotta other guys, an' there I was lookin' out in the audience, which had about fifty other pugs sittin' there, an' they're all starin' at me, smilin', and I'm starin' back at them an' smilin'. And the speaker, whose face looked like he had been through two hundred tough scraps, was talkin' 'bout me. He was sayin' nice things about the neighborhood I come from an' how I done it on my own an' all that kind of stuff. "Rocky Balboa," the speaker said, "is now a member of the Cauliflower Alley Club! Long live the Rock!"

I stood, and for a second I wished Rocky Marciano were alive. I just thought about that great guy. He had been my idol an' I would have liked to see his face, knowing that I had brought a little more honor to his great name. I walked toward the stand an' the speaker brought up this giant cauliflower ear, which was supposed to be a trophy, an' he handed it to me. I held up the ear to the side of my head an' everybody laughed a little bit, and then I lowered it down and started to talk to my fellow brothers out there.

"Thanks. I'm happy for this honor an' I'd like to do somethin' for other fighters who never got no break," I said an' pulled out this check from my pocket. "I wanna give ya guys this check for five thousand to start buildin' a retirement home for ex-fighters . . . Y'know, we all need one."

Now somethin' special was happenin'—the old high school I was throwed outta was now givin' me this here special diploma. The whole school was there. Boy, was I excited.

"And to Robert 'Rocky' Balboa, a former student . . . a man they called a million-to-one shot, Lincoln High School is proud to present you with an honorary diploma."

God, everybody jumped up an' started yellin' my name. I looked at Adrian an' she was cryin' a little.

"I ain't sure—excuse me—I'm not sure what to say. I retired from school in ninth grade, y'know, to be a fighter, so it took me, I dunno, 'bout seventeen years and a lot of beatin's to get this . . . so my advice to ya's is get it while it's hot, y'know . . . I want, I mean . . . thanks."

Adrian started complainin' when I was slippin' these gold bracelets on her wrist. We was standin' in the jewelry store that we used to pass all the time when we was stone broke, only now I could afford to walk in there and act like a real customer. An' I was doin' my best to do so. Adrian sighed an' just watched me put more gold bracelets on her, an' finally she smiled. I was hopin' the saleslady would say somethin' that would make me look important. I was hopin' she'd say, "My, what a big spender." Instead, the saleslady asked if it was cash or charge.

Adrian and I was standin' outside this woman's coat place, and again it was one of them stores that we could never afford to walk into a couple months ago, but now we could. I was askin' Adrian if she liked the coat in the window, and she kept shakin' her head "no," but I knew she wasn't tellin' the truth. She was still shakin' her head when I pulled her into the store.

Now it was my turn to spend a little bread on myself. I could have gone into Center City or some of the sharper shops, but I decided to go down to the place where I used to pick up a pair of pants or a sweater now and then, and the place was called South Street. South Street was really somethin'. I don't know if any other cities got places like South Street, but on South Street, you could be walkin' along the sidewalk and somebody would snatch you into the store and start tellin' you how you couldn't live without a pair of his pants; then you pulled yourself away an' somebody else'd snatch you into another shop and say, "How could you survive without a new pair of shoes?" So even if you had a dollar in your pocket and you had nothin' to do, y'could always just walk down South Street an' be snatched into stores all day long. You may not end up buying nothin', but at least ya feel wanted.

But like I said, here I was in a South Street clothing shop and I had on this suit. It weren't a quiet suit, it was a loud suit. I had a feelin' I looked kinda gross in this suit, but I didn't feel like tryin' nothin' else on, 'cause I wanted it to be like it was, you know, in them fantasy books. Like Cinderella and the slipper. I wanted the same thing to happen to me. I wanted to walk into the shop, put on one suit, and feel like Gregory Peck or somebody like that no matter how bad it looked. So rather than blow my fantasy, I just said to the salesman, "Perfect! Five more of the same color, please."

I was sittin' in the back seat of this Ford sedan with Adrian and Butkus when it pulled up along this house for sale on Lambert Street in South Philly. Adrian an' me was thinkin' about buyin' a house in Fishtown, since I'd lived there so long an' kinda owed the neighborhood a little bit of loyalty, but Fishtown was havin' its problems. It seems like every day someone would tear another building down, so why buy a house an' have somebody come

along an' smash it? I figured the smart move would
be to go to South Philadelphia, where there was a
lot of Italians, an' I figured maybe a few of my
ancestors musta lived around there, too. So why not
keep it in the family, right?

Even though it was kinda cold, they still had a
few kids playin' stick ball on the nice street. And
it was a nice street. They even had a couple trees
here an' there and no writin' on the wall. There were
none of them dirty words scribbled on bricks to
make you feel like ya just been walkin' through a
bus-station toilet. That's what I think about every
time I see graffiti on the wall. Every time I see
graffiti I think that some guy, some crazy guy, has
gotten out of the Greyhound Bus Station bathroom
with a Magic Marker or somethin' and has been let
loose in the streets. It was like if he couldn't bring
the city to the Greyhound Bus Station graffiti toilets,
he was gonna bring the Greyhound Bus Station
graffiti to the city. It was an epidemic.

Anyway, I patted Butkus on the side of the head
an' took Adrian's hand and we got out of the real-
estate guy's dark Ford and went into the house.

The agent was down in the basement with me and
Adrian, lookin' around. He was tryin' to show us
the nice furnace an' the water heater and all that
kind of stuff an' how these walls wouldn't leak because they'd just been sealed with some new kinda
plastic stuff made by DuPont or Elmer's Glue or
one of them sticky companies. Adrian was askin' all
the questions 'cause I was in the mood to daydream.
I was just lookin' around and daydreamin' and
thinkin' about all the things I could do with this
house if it were mine.

"Does it have copper plumbing?" Adrian asked.
"Yes indeed," the agent answered.

I was lookin' around, and then I seen it. Something so perfect that I had to tell Adrian about it right away. This I couldn't keep in. "Yo, Adrian, there's a great place to hang a bag! I gotta teach you to work the bag, you'll love it."

Adrian smiled at me again an' we started following this agent upstairs. He was an old guy, and a couple of times I almost felt maybe I should give him a little boost up the last few steps.

He was explainin' the layout an' Adrian was listenin' real close, but me, my mind was elsewhere. I just wanted that man to leave so I could get involved with livin' there.

"The house is structured with steel support and the floors are oak," the agent said.

I pointed to a corner and said, "That's a good spot for a TV." I guess no one thought it was a very bright statement, 'cause nobody looked at me when I said it.

"What're the taxes a year?" Adrian asked.

"Fifteen hundred."

I was gettin' tired of this business talk goin' back and forth, so I just turned to the agent and said, "Y'know, I like it. Adrian, I know a great deal when I see one!"

"Rocky, you're making this man's job very easy."

Sure I was makin' the guy's job easy. This was a house, and it was the only house I could ever walk into and say I'd like to buy, so why would I cause trouble?

"We'll take it," I said, and leaned close to the agent and pretended to be mad. "And it'd better not leak, or else!"

The agent didn't know if I was crazy, but he figured I was just joking, 'cause he smiled a little bit and looked around for the door. I guess the agent figured that me and Adrian wanted to be alone, 'cause we was just staring at him, so he drifted out of the room an' I touched Adrian's arm an' leaned against the stairs in the house that we just bought. "Y'know, Adrian, I feel dumb talkin' like this with the lights on . . . I gotta say somethin'. What I gotta say is that none of this stuff—the house, the plumbin'—none of this means nothin' without you—'cause without ya bein' here, I wouldn't be here . . . I hope you can make sense outta that."

Adrian put her fingers against my lips an' said, "You don't have to speak."

Sweat was pouring off the champion as he drove punch after punch into the heavy bag. The large leather cylinder sang every time it was attacked by Apollo Creed's lightning jabs and swift hooks. His trainer seemed to be riding on the back of some berserk bucking animal as he strained to hold the heavy bag still as the champion continued his relentless assault.

"Time!" the trainer yelled in an almost pleading manner.

Apollo Creed was deaf to the words, because, rather than stopping and taking a well-earned breather, he stepped up his assault. He continued to pound
and pound
and pound some more.

"Is it a boy or a girl?" I asked as we walked across this park.

"Oh, Rocky, the doctor can't tell yet."

"Jeez, how do you feel? Different? Like heavier?"

"No, I feel just fine, but I can't believe I'm havin' a baby."

"I'll tell ya, I want him to have your good brain an' looks an' my left hook—he'll really be somethin' . . . Oh, no! What if it's a broad—sorry, I mean girl?"

"Well, I hope she won't be shy like me. We'll give her singing and dancing lessons."

I jumped in. "An' a new dress every day—an' she'll need a bodyguard at school to keep the boys away. Y'know how boys are in general."

"I want her to be like her father."

I laughed. "Don't ya think one dumbbell in the family is enough? . . . I swear, I ain't gonna let this kid hang on no corners, or get no tattoos, or dress like no wise guy like me . . . He's gonna be a good somebody like you!"

"No, like you!"

"Like you!"

I hugged her and yelled as loud as I could, "Yo, Adrian, we did it!"

16

WELL, THE BIG day was finally here. I was sittin'
in this chair havin' all this makeup thrown on by a
guy they call a makeup man. The man himself was
kind of a lightweight, if you know what I mean. He
was kind of half-man, half-gumdrop. As he was
puttin' this powder an' stuff all over my face, gettin'
me ready for my big start in commercials, he was
shakin' his rear to some sorta disco music comin'
outta his small tape recorder. Yeah, he was havin'
a great old time shakin' his butt and splashin' makeup on me.

I smiled at Adrian an' thought she looked even
better now that she was four months' pregnant and
startin' to show. Yeah, everything in my life was
comin' up aces. The two agents, Short and Shorter,
was standin' in the doorway smokin' cigarettes and
walkin' back and forth lookin' at their watches.

"Listen," the short agent said, "we're sorry it
took a couple months to get ya here, but the spon-
sors wanted to make sure all the swelling was gone."

"That's right," the shorter agent said.

"Sure . . . listen, ya think the stuff will be written on them cards?" I asked.

"For sure . . . Is he ready?" the short agent said to the makeup man.

"Finito," the makeup man said and turned off his cassette recorder.

I don't know, I think I looked kinda stupid, so I turned to Adrian and asked, "How do I look?"

"Pretty good," she lied.

I did look like a jerk. For some reason these guys took me out of my normal clothes and put me in some costume. I was dressed like Tarzan with bones around my neck and this big rubber club.

My hair, which usually looked curly, was now all flattened by this tiger-striped headband and looked dumb. I thought I should be in a tree in the park. I held Adrian's arm.

"Don't get nervous," Adrian said.

"I look very stupid, don't I?"

"Yes."

". . . got any deodorant?"

I was walkin' from the dressing room to the stage they had set up with all these bright lights. It kinda reminded me of a miniature ball park gettin' ready for a night game.

Soon as some of the assistants saw me comin', they didn't waste no time an' took me by the hand and sat me in a chair and got all these microphones adjusted, then from behind the camera come this guy they call the director. He was kinda skinny, kinda stumpy, and also had kind of a skinny, short beard and tiny, narrow eyes.

"All right, Rocky, let's get it together," the director said. "You know the routine, Rocky. Just like we rehearsed, right? Right! We're running late. All right, let's get it together."

It was like one of them submarine movies when everyone hit their battle stations and was ready to fire a torpedo any second.

"Ready," the director said.

"Speed here."

"Rolling!"

"Action!" the director said.

Well, here I go. And I was ready. I just hope they hold them cue cards still. "In the morning—I—splash—it—on—and—it does—smeal—mainly . . ."

"Cut!" the director said and sounded mad. "Smeal mainly?! Smell manly; the words are smell manly . . . Once again, Rocky."

"Excuse me."

"Yes?"

"I know I said it wrong, but it really don't smell manly. D'ya think this stuff smells like a man? I'd say absolutely no."

"Want to try it again?"

"Sure, but it still don't smell like no man. It kinda reminds me of fruit punch, don't it, Adrian?"

". . . yes."

"Want to try it again?"

". . . sorry."

"Action!"

". . . I splash it on and it—does—mainly—sorry . . . manly things to—me. It—surrounds—my—face—with—class."

"Cut!" the director said and hit the arm of his chair. "The word is *class*. Do you know the word *class?* . . . It's in the dictionary. The way you slur it, it sounds like *crass* or *glass* or *ass!* That's no good, Rocky—no good! The word is definitely *class!*" he said very loud and shook his head in disgust.

Adrian walked forward and touched his arm. "Excuse me . . . he'd do better if he had his glasses."

"Whoever you are, thank you for your advice, but I know my business," the director said in a rude way.

I was hopin' that he wouldn't get any more rude, because one more rude word and I would have to step in and do something unnecessary. Lucky he didn't say no more rude things to Adrian and turned to his camera guy. "All right, picture up . . . Never mind!" I knew this wouldn't work. "Get 'im ready for the alternate layout." The director turned to one of the agents and said, "Thanks to your client, the whole morning's a bust!" The director went over and poured himself what looked to me like a glass of wine and lit a cigarette. Well, almost lit a cigarette; someone else jumped in there with a match first. I guess that was his job.

I really felt bad. I felt bad for Adrian 'cause I was so embarrassing. I got outta the chair and started walking toward the dressing room. "Y'know, Adrian, it sounded great inside before it came out."

The champion was shadowboxing in front of a mirror completely embroidered with stains of toil. Streams of sweat and mucus ran down over his reflected image. The more he shadowboxed, the more intense his eyes became on striving to reach a personal goal that only he could understand. His trainer came forward and threw a towel over the champion's shoulder and said, "Let's take a break." Apollo Creed shrugged the towel from his shoulders and continued to work, and work, and work.

This time these guys had gone to a whole different kind of expense. This time these guys bought some boxing stuff and made me get into it, then they hauled me back to the makeup guy again and he really done a job on my face. He covered me with about a ton of bruises and welts and made my nose look like swollen sausage, worse than when Creed had flattened it against the side of my face.

I didn't want to look at Adrian 'cause I knew how really embarrassed she must be to see me like this, so I just looked straight ahead at this small ring they had set up for me. Behind the ring was this painting with a lot of cartoon people cheerin' an' stuff like that.

The agents were standin' near the ring, an' when I give 'em a look, they give me back the "okay" sign like everythin' was gonna be hunky-dory. But this weren't the way I figured commercials was shot. I thought, like when you did a dog-food commercial, somebody hands you a can and turns some dog loose on ya, and you pat the dog's head and say, "See how great this dog is from eatin' this junk"; then ya pick up your money and you go home. This was gettin' confusin'.

Adrian come over and touched my robe. When I turned around, I could hardly see her outta my right eye 'cause they had covered it with some kinda plastic. I swear, if they'd put antennas on my head I coulda been in one of them space movies. That's how bad I looked. "Rocky, you don't have to go through with this," Adrian said.

"It's okay. I got nothin' else to do this afternoon." I seen the little director come forward and stomp his foot on the stage like he was ten years old.

"All right, wet him down! Move!" he said and lit up another cigarette.

This other makeup man with long hair and a lot of bracelets come up to me and started sprayin' my face with water, and I had to admit I did look like I was sweatin'. Now I really looked bad. It's one thing to be beat up and dry-lookin', but when you're beat up and wet-lookin' you become a very slimy guy in general. This afternoon was gettin' pathetic for me.

"Ready!" the director shouted.

"Rolling . . ."

"Speed."

The stick guy come forward and said, "Beast After-Shave . . . The Contender . . . Take one!" and he slammed the sticks down.

"Try to get it right, Rocky," the director said. "Action!"

This young guy with glasses was holdin' up a stack of cue cards. Cue cards! I must be gettin' the hang of this show-biz talkin'. There I was lookin' at the cue cards, and I smiled inside 'cause I knew now everythin' was gonna be okay.

"Hi . . . my—name—is—Rocky—Balboa, the— Italian Stallion. I—am the American dream—but not . . . Yo, can I do it over please, Mr. Director?"

"Christ! Cut!" the director yelled and shook his head. "Look, just read the dummy cards!"

Now I was turnin' very red! But still I was more embarrassed for Adrian than for me. You know, here I was, her husband, the guy she's supposed to be proud of, and I was being embarrassed by this little stranger. Some people just ain't great at some things, but if they give it their best shot, no one should ever yell at them.

The makeup man with the jinglin' bracelets come over again and started wettin' my face and back and arms, and before I knew it I was drippin'.

"Speed up, let's go!" the director said. "All right, action!"

"Hi . . . My—name—is—Rocky Balboa—the Italian Stallion. They say—I'm the American dream —but—I'm not . . ." I said, but couldn't believe what I was saying. I had a feeling that I wasn't sellin' Beast Cologne, but I think I was sellin' out instead. "After—a hard day—in the ring, I don't look like the American dream, I look like—the American scream . . . Then I say, Rocky boy, you gotta shape up. Then I slap on this Beast After Shave," I said, and I could feel my voice beginnin' to crack. For a few bucks I was makin' a fool of myself. Everythin' I'd worked for was now bein' used as a joke for some cologne. "Then I really am —the American dream—so don't be—punchy . . . So don't be punchy—like—me . . . Don't be . . . Be a smart guy—and . . ." I stopped and looked at the director, who was chewin' on the end of a pencil, and said, "Y'know, I ain't punchy, I got what ya call a relaxed brain—it's just the way I talk."

"What's the difference?"

"This ain't right—this whole thing ain't right."

"What isn't?!"

"You're a rude guy. I'm tryin' hard an' you're bein' rude. That's bad manners, ain't it, Adrian?" I said and turned to her.

"Yes," Adrian said and looked at the director.

"You want to quit, then quit! I didn't want you in the first place! You're a waste of time—you can't even read!"

I walked over to the director and grabbed him. I pulled off some of this thick makeup they had covered my face with and poured some Beast After Shave on the director's head.

"Ya got the wrong name for this stuff—ya oughta call it Creep Cologne!"

"Somebody call security!" the director yelled and tried to squirm away.

"You're a rude guy," I said and handed him the bottle of after-shave. I think he was yellin' some pretty high-class curse words at me, but I didn't pay no attention, and with Adrian I left the world of commercials behind.

"It does smell like fruit punch, don't it?" I said.

"I'm proud of you," Adrian said.

"Thanks . . . Thank you."

17

APOLLO CREED SAT in his living room. Beside him was a large stack of mail that overflowed from a canvas bag and onto the floor. Several pieces even covered his shoe. Apollo Creed did not pay any attention to the television or the noise his two children created playing upstairs. His wife was the only one who had Apollo's attention, a twenty-nine-year-old statuesque beauty who had met Apollo when he was a young sparring partner for a former light-heavyweight champion. She had met him when everyone with whom he came in contact had said, "That's all he'll ever be—a fancy fly-by-night show-boating sparring partner." The boy was good, but he clowned too much. He was great for laughs. Supposedly when she met Apollo Creed, he was doomed to be the proverbial gymnasium humorist. History proved otherwise. The detractors never considered his tremendous pride.

Apollo unfolded another letter and threw the envelope down in disgust and read, " 'You didn't beat nobody, and anybody who knows boxing knows the fight was fixed . . .' " Apollo turned to his wife. "Listen to this one: 'You call yourself a champ, but you're a fake. Go kill yourself.' " Apollo dropped the letter onto the growing stack and rubbed his forehead as though some great wave of exhaustion had overtaken the muscles of his face.

"That's me they're talkin' about," he said.

"Why can't you ignore it?"

Apollo looked at her for a very long moment, and the hurt rose from his stomach into his eyes. He dropped the letters to the floor and stared hard at his hands.

Y'know, I was really gettin' glad that the weather was changin', because when the weather gets warm I feel like my blood starts to flow through places in my body that have been locked up during the winter. I feel like my body sometimes is like one of them empty ballrooms that closed down for certain seasons, and it feels like just an empty old warehouse along Delaware Avenue. Then when the warm weather hits town, all of a sudden that ballroom fills and I feel like a million bucks. I think turtles feel that way, too. They move more in warm weather, that's a fact.

I was playin' stickball with the Manetti brothers and three other kids. Stickball's always been one of my favorites. If they ever had professional stickball, I had a shot at goin' pro, but it never caught on.

Not even in Japan.

I ran my hand up and down the broomstick and got the feel of this bat an' waited for the half-ball to come floating past. Bobby Manetti wound up and I seen the half-ball leave his hand an' float toward the sewer top we was using for home plate. Oh boy, this one was goin' to the moon. I cranked back, tensed my legs, straightened my back, leveled my wrist, and swung.

I missed.

That's impossible!

I miss a lot of things in life but I never miss at stickball. Bobby laughed and pitched a second time, and I swung, and the only thing I did was help fan the neighborhood. I covered my left eye and looked at Bobby Manetti standin' on the pitcher's mound and I could see the problem right away. Well, I could almost see the problem; the problem was I couldn't hardly see. Y'know, I really liked Apollo Creed, but he did mess up my eye pretty bad. It was like somebody was hangin' a slab of dirty Jello over my eye. I had a hard time seein' anything. I didn't worry about it too much, I know it'd get better. It just needed some time to heal, right?

Bobby wound up and pitched again, but this time I was ready for him, so I kinda made up for the blurred eyes by leanin' a little bit more to the left an' smacked it hard. Some people like the sound of a champagne cork flyin' an' smackin' against the ceiling. Some people like the sound of racin' cars revving their engines. Me, I'll take the sound of a half-ball bein' hit with a splintered broomstick sailing ten cars down the block. I was in heaven! I tossed the bat to Bobby and said, "Now I know the day weren't no waste. C'mon, you guys, take a shot. I gotta go home an' eat."

"Yo, Rocky, come on, hit another one," Bobby said.

I was about to oblige when Adrian leaned her head out the window, half a block away, and called to me, "Rocky! Dinner!"

"Well, looks like you guys gotta get along without me," I said.

"That ain't hard," Bobby said and laughed.

I messed up his hair and kinda sparred with him for a second and started to jog home.

I dropped down into my chair and looked at the platter of spaghetti an' chicken wings that was layin' in front of me. I didn't bother to use my napkin, 'cause I never did. I was such a sloppy eater that a napkin wouldn't help at all. I was hopin' that someday a smart guy would invent a whole bag that would go over your body and just leave a hole for your mouth. That's the kind of napkin I needed.

Adrian had my glasses next to the plate, so I put 'em on and the world become a clear place again. Old Butkus was sittin' next to me, droolin' as usual. He was always a droolin' creature, so I give him three or four strands of spaghetti. "Yo, Butkus, open your mouth . . ." I said and turned to my wife. "Y'know, Adrian, I don't think I'm gonna make no giant name in commercials."

"Rocky, nobody should treat people like you were treated."

"That's true," I said and bent down and started feedin' Butkus off my plate with a fork. Why not? Butkus is part of the family.

"Rocky, you shouldn't do that, you'll get germs."

"I'll gargle . . . Y'know, it looks easy . . . makin' commercials. All you gotta do is talk, right? Y'know, maybe I coulda done better if I'd worn my glasses . . ." I felt like I was lyin' a little bit, because I think if I had worn ten pairs of glasses it wouldn't've got no better. I'm just not cut out for brainy things.

I looked at Adrian, and she did look great sittin' over there. "Y'know, you look great sittin' over there."

"You're not so bad yourself."

Well, that's all I had to hear, and I was outta my seat and over to her and huggin' her tight against me.

"What a family we're gonna have . . . Don't worry about nothin', tomorrow's gonna be a great day, Adrian."

This was my first day on the street, and I wasn't gettin' anywhere. I figured I'd walk into an office and people'd say, "Hey, I saw you on television. I'd like to have you around in my office. How would you like a desk to sit down at? How would you like a typewriter? How would you like a secretary? How'd you like a coffee break?" You know, all them things that go along with bein' a big office guy. But none of that were happenin'. This was the fourth employment office I'd been to and it wasn't even twelve o'clock yet. All the employment offices seemed the same. They were all painted with the same kind of green paint and they all felt the same.

I was sittin' across from this chubby, stubby guy who was probably about thirty-nine, forty years old. His skin wasn't white any more, it was kinda gray. Matter of fact, I think it was kinda light green, like the walls. He was becomin' part of the buildin', he'd been sittin' there so long. And I guess I kinda looked a little stiff myself, 'cause I wasn't used to sittin' in a suit all day. I could feel the back of my legs sweatin' and startin' to grow onto the chair.

". . . and how far did you go in high school, Mr. Balboa?"

"Ninth."

"I have one last question. Do you have a criminal record?"

"Ah, nothin' worth braggin' about."

"Would you consider any sort of manual labor?"

"There's nothing wrong with honest work, y'know. But I'd like to see if I can make a livin' sittin' down like you."

"Can I be honest? No one's going to offer you an office job, there's too much competition. Why don't you fight? You're a good fighter."

I stood up and felt myself gettin' a little hot under the collar. Yeah, this guy was right. I'd been a fighter all my life, but that's not what I wanted to be no more. That's what I had to do to get along an' make a buck without becomin' a professional bum, or something like that. And here's this guy who didn't know what he was talkin' about, tellin' me to go back and be somethin' I didn't want to be.

"Was ya ever punched in the face five hundred times a night?" I asked the guy, "It stings after a while." I left.

Apollo Creed tapped his gloves together and drove another straight left, followed by a stinging right, into a large sparring partner's semi-covered face. Apollo moved with incredible intensity as he banged away, and away, and away. Apollo was no longer a regular man; he was becoming a machine in satin shorts.

I stood in front of another guy and shook hands with this thin man who was sittin' behind the desk. The suit I was wearing still looked pretty good, except for the wrinkles around the crotch area, but that's to be expected, I suppose. He had a little mirror on the wall across from the desk, and I caught a glimpse of myself. I thought I kinda resembled a sissy. I think I spent too much time this mornin' with the comb and hair tonic. The man rubbed this shiny spot he had between his eyebrows and said, ". . . I'm very sorry, Rocky. I only wish you had the qualifications for the job you want."

"Y'know anybody who needs a doorman?" I said and smiled. "I'm just kiddin'."

I was gettin' what you might call an empty tank inside. I was feelin' tense an' empty. I was sittin' in another employment office in front of another man with another head of gray hair, and he was about to tell me the same thing. I knew he was gonna talk about high school, an' I knew he was gonna talk about opportunities and diplomas and qualifications. I think these guys all graduated from the same school of excuses.

"Mr. Balboa . . . you have to be realistic. No high-school diploma, no qualifications. Don't you think you'd be more content in a good-paying menial job?" He picked up a list that was on his desk. "There's an opportunity as a baker's assistant. It pays well. Can you bake?"

"No, just boil," I said and headed for the doorknob.

The champion was still dissecting his large sparring partner. He laced into the man with a vicious combination of punches directed more at the punishment aspect of fighting rather than at the quick kill. When he realized he had his sparring partner on the brink of unconsciousness, he unleashed a blurring combination that dropped the man cold. Apollo just stared at the man as his mind raced ahead.

18

SOME OF THE streets were gettin' hotter and hotter and filled with more noise every night. I was so used to these streets 'cause all my life I'd done everythin' but eat off 'em. Sometimes I had almost done even that. I knew every brick, every crack, every rusting El-train bolt. I knew where every dirty word was written on every wall in the neighborhood. If anyone ever wanted a guided tour through Fishtown, I was their man.

Fishtown was kinda buzzin' with excitement tonight because a couple of guys had been shot over at Lucky's Bar, about five blocks from where I used to live. I doubt if they would ever catch the guys who done it, 'cause nobody talks to the cops in Fishtown.

They only talk to each other,
and half the time
they only tell half of
what they know.

I was startin' to get the feel of Fishtown back into my blood. It was a neighborhood that kinda looked the way I felt inside, y'know. It had moods good and bad and some in between, but mostly there was a survivin' mood about the neighborhood, an' that's the way I felt about myself. To survive, I figured I had to go back to what I was. I couldn't keep puttin' on these monkey suits an' walkin' around in people's offices an' havin' them tell me I'm not good enough to be one of them, so now I was sittin' in the back of Gazzo's black Cadillac. Paulie was behind the wheel and sneakin' glances at me in the rear-view mirror. I was wearin' my old hat an' had put on my glasses, 'cause what was there to hide any more? But I didn't like regular people seein' me with glasses on, not that I had anything against glasses, it's just that I was one of the few people in the world who would put on glasses and look more stupid with 'em than without 'em.

"So what d'ya wanna do?" Gazzo asked.

"I wanna fight, but Adrian don't wanna know from me fightin', and I don't want her gettin' upset, 'cause I got a family on the way. Yo, Paulie, she says she's gonna go to work at the Pet Shop again, y'know, part-time."

"That dumbhead," Paulie said.

"Yo, don't be sayin' that."

I guess Gazzo got tired of hearing us always jumpin' on each other, so he just rubbed his two hands together, then eyed Butkus sittin' in the rear. I loved my dog, Adrian loved this dog, but Gazzo, he'd like to see this dog made into a bath mat or a pair of gloves. Gazzo would've made a lousy Boy Scout or anything else that dealt in nature. If it has fur, Gazzo wanted to be either wearing it or standin' on it, not pettin' it.

"Hey, Rock, this is the last time I want that dog sittin' in my car," Gazzo said.

"Yeah, it's bad for the rep," Paulie added.

Gazzo lit another cigarette. "Yeah, very bad. Listen, I like you, Rock—you weren't the best collector I ever had—"

"He was trustworthy," Paulie said.

"Yeah, trustworthy. Look, let me put you on the street again. Forget these straight jobs, they'll only confuse you."

"I think you gotta go back to fightin'," Paulie said.

Gazzo gave Paulie a pretty hot look for interruptin'. Gazzo didn't know that Paulie was a born interrupter and that no hot looks or anything else was gonna make him polite.

"Yeah," I said, "but I can't upset Adrian when she's pregnant, y'know?"

"Paulie, why don't you take the Rock to the club —I own a piece of it, Rocky. I want you to look it over, and if you like it—"

Paulie interrupted again. "And if you like it, we'll put you in as a bouncer."

Gazzo gave Paulie another hot look as Paulie flipped the Cadillac into gear and we began to ooze our way through Fishtown.

19

I WAS ABOUT a block away when I could hear the music start comin' into my head. It was that disco-sound music. I liked this disco music 'cause it made you want to get out and move your feet, and that kinda reminded me of roadwork, so I figured it had to be healthy, y'know? My favorite kinda music, though, was gettin' four or five guys drunk on fifty-cent wine and doin' a cappella on any street corner in Philly on a cold night. That was music 'cause them guys was singin' just for themselves. As we started to get close to the blinkin' lights and the sign out front, Paulie inched ahead of me like he was leading the way. I noticed Paulie had lost a lot of weight in the past few months, and I think it was good. Now he was thin. He didn't look like two people with one head no more.

"Maybe you'll dance some—it'd be good for you and my sister to dance a little, what d'ya think? It'll make you forget everything else," Paulie said and lit a cigarette.

"I got bad ankles."

"Then you can snap your fingers. Hey, my sister givin' you a hard time?"

"A little, y'know."

Paulie spit an' snapped his fingers. "Soon I'll talk with her. If she don't listen to me I'll punch her lights out!" Paulie said and walked inside the swirling lights.

Boy, I ain't never seen nothin' like this. The music was so loud I thought my ears were gonna swell an' explode an' I'd be standin' there with just two black, smokin' holes on the side of my head. I ain't never heard no music that loud before. And the lights! Whoever put those lights together must be pretty smart, 'cause it reminded me of a spaceship, or somethin' from a dream you have at night. The lights looked so good I wanted to reach up and touch 'em, or taste them or do what I was doin' and just stare at 'em. I was really happy I was standin' here, because I felt like I was in a playground for people about my age. Always used to think about that. Y'know, where does a guy go to play when he gets past twenty-five or thirty? Does he just drink a little beer and play a little cards with the guys, and take a stroll once in a while? That ain't right, so somebody invented these throbbin', light-spinnin', smoky, choky playgrounds for people who don't feel like gettin' old.

I really wish I could dance. I really wish God didn't give me dead feet and instead had laid some great footwork on me, like Apollo Creed has. I woulda been a real tornado, but since I had the worst case of bad rhythm in the world, I just had to settle for tappin' my fingers on the side of my leg.

"Nice place, ain't it?" Paulie said. "What flavor you like? Blonde, brunettes, mixed grill?"

"I like the way Adrian looks," I said.

Paulie laughed and touched my chest with his short finger. "Then maybe we oughta be at a freak show!"

"Hey, don't say that!"

"Just kiddin'. Don't go gettin' mental, Rock," Paulie said and looked around. "Y'know, bein' a bouncer in here would be easy work, you could settle down to an easy life . . . See anybody you wanna bounce?" Paulie said and laughed. Paulie headed for two girls who was leanin' against the bar . . . I remember them bein' different from most of the girls I seen on the streets. They was dressed with a lot of, ah, what do you call it? Flash! Yeah, they were sharp! One looked kinda young and was tryin' to age herself by splashin' on makeup and stuff. She was probably pretty cute under all the war paint, and the other one was about six feet tall, I'd say. She looked like she was in good shape and had long, long arms. I'd say her reach was at least seventy-four inches; of course, that's just an estimate off the top of my head.

Paulie touched my arm an' nodded toward the tall girl. "I can't stand tall broads. I used to go out with a tall broad, three years ago come August. Tall, she was, a skyscraper among broads. And every time she come down to kiss my mouth, I'd think of some crap TV show I seen about big birds feedin' little birds worms, y'know?"

"So what d'ya got against birds, Paulie?"

"I don't like friggin' birds or worms," Paulie yelled.

I nodded just to make him cool down, but I didn't know where Paulie was coming from. Sometimes I think Paulie fell off a spaceship or somethin', 'cause he didn't resemble nobody else I ever seen on this planet. He had his own way of talkin' an' thinkin'

an' lousin' up things. Paulie was gonna do somethin' stupid, I had a feelin'; then I was sure he was
gonna do somethin' stupid when I seen him walkin'
toward the two girls. He stopped in front of them
and eyed the short one, then the tall one, then back
to the short one again, wiped his lips with the back
of his hand, and said, "I'm Paulie . . . this is
Rocky."

Both them girls said nothing, and I couldn't
blame 'em. Paulie was very annoyed to hear nothin'
comin' outta their mouths and he kinda got a little
hot.

"Rocky here can punch out anybody in the house,
you wanna see?"

I could see the girls gettin' nervous an' wantin'
to get outta there, but Paulie inched his way a little
closer. You may find this hard to believe, but I
think Paulie really thought he was a real lover type
and these girls was eatin' up all he had to say.
Sometimes bein' with Paulie is about as much fun
as findin' a strange hair in your food, y'know.

"Are you two broads married?" Paulie asked.
"Any kids on the way?"

Them girls shook their heads "no" and tried to
move away, but Paulie blocked them off. "Go on,
Rock, talk . . . ask 'em anything you want—that's
what they're here for, right, girls? Go on, Rock,
don't be shy," Paulie said and smiled at the girls,
then looked back at me. "He's gonna run this dump
soon."

I was hopin' I could just disappear into the
poundin' music and blinkin' lights and smoke, but I
didn't think I was gonna get my wish. Paulie lit up
a cigarette an' pointed to me again. "Go on, Rock,
ask the broads a friggin' question."

Now I was really on the spot. I didn't know what

to say, so I just looked at the taller girl and asked, "What's your height?" For some reason the girls looked at me like I was a real sicko and moved away. Paulie had been insulting them for ten minutes and they hung around; I said one thing and they both peeled out. I think this is how people get them bad personality complexes . . . I think.

Paulie was kinda mad at me and said, "Why didn't you ask her weight, too? What, Rock, did you wanna spar her?"

"Yo, Paulie, I don't know any good questions . . . Maybe I oughta forget this place."

I was really tryin' to forget this place when the bartender leaned over and interrupted my thinking.

"What'll it be?"

"A shot of Canadian for me. What d'ya want, Rock?"

I usually drink beer, but I figured in a place like this I should have somethin' a little bit different, so instead of takin' up a lot of the bartender's time, I turned and looked at this guy, I think it was a guy . . . I looked at this guy in a flowered shirt sittin' at the bar sippin' a drink that looked like it was made out of melted crayons.

"I'll have one of 'em," I said.

The bartender nodded. "A shot of Canadian for you and a Pink Lady for you." A Pink Lady for me! Was he talkin' to me? Pink Lady? That could be impossible, I think. I watched the bartender move away and I felt very embarrassed, and I was gonna tell Paulie I ain't holdin' no Pink Lady drink.

"Yo, Paulie, I ain't holdin' no Pink Lady drink."

"Put a napkin around it—I won't tell nobody."

"I'm gettin' outta here," I said.

The bartender come over and put the Pink Lady next to the guy, the skinny guy in the flowered shirt, and I leaned over and picked up the drink and walked over to the tall girl. I gotta admit she was tall, I figured six feet tall. I was still tryin' to guess her height, like they do at the carnival, when she caught my eye and tried to move off into a dark corner. I walked around the edge of the dance floor because I didn't wanna be trapped out there, and cut her off as she rounded the other side of the dance floor.

"Yo . . . excuse me, could ya stop your feet? . . . I just wanna say to ya I didn't mean nothin'. I didn't want ya to think I was tryin' to be wise, 'cause bein' wise ain't what I come here for. Paulie, my friend over there, brought me here in case I wanted to be a bouncer. I need the bread 'cause Adrian, my wife, who is his kid sister, is gonna have a kid, and we need the dough. So I just wanted ya to know I was here on business and weren't tryin' to be wise . . . Sorry."

I handed this tall girl the Pink Lady drink and started to move away, but I felt some words comin' up from my stomach, so I turned around, opened my mouth, and let 'em come out. "This is for you. Y'know, you should be happy bein' tall, 'cause ya get the clean air first."

Paulie musta heard what I said, 'cause he was smilin' and standin' a couple feet behind me.

"That's a crazy thing to say," Paulie said. "Yo, Rock, you goin' crazy or somethin'? Ya shoulda whacked her out."

"Paulie, did ya ever think about seein' a head doctor?"

"No, why?"

"Forget it. See ya later."

I left.

20

THE SIGN IN front of Mickey's gym sure needed a paint job bad, and if I had the money I would give it to him. I always wondered about things like that. People get a good idea and they paint a proud sign like this one with Mickey standin' there about fifteen feet tall, in a ring, strikin' up a fancy boxin' pose, and all the letters are drawn real fancy-like, and then they just let the whole thing fall apart. Boy, if it were my sign I would go up there at least once every six months, if the weather was right, and touch it up, but it weren't my sign, so all I could do was think about it.

I opened up my wallet and took out this key that I had tucked away in the spot that you usually use for credit cards, and I opened the gym door. I waved for my dog to follow me in, and he did just that and we started climbin' the stairs. If I was blindfolded and put in this place, I'd know exactly where I was no matter what. The smell of somethin' that burns into ya' nose, ya might say. It's the thick smell of sweat an' pain an' dried blood an' things that hurt. I don't wanna think about it no more 'cause I'll get depressed.

Butkus and I were walkin' up the steps when suddenly I seen somethin' silver move through the blackness at the top of the steps and smash against the wall. My heart jumped about a foot and I heard this roaring voice come rollin' down at me.

"Who the hell is it?!"

Good old Mickey, he'll never change. Mickey stood with his lead pipe held like a baseball bat, and I covered my bad eye so I could focus in on him. He looked funny and dangerous both at the same time, standin' there in his underwear and tank-top undershirt, with his long, ugly lead pipe just waitin' to put a crease in anybody's skull.

"Who the hell is it?" he said.

"The Avon Lady," I said.

"Rocky? I don't remember givin' you a key. What the hell are you doin'? Come up here, Rock."

I accepted the invite an' started to move up the steps with ol' Butkus. Now that I was standin' close, I could get a good look at Mickey. He looked pretty good, I had to admit. Maybe he'd been eatin' better lately, or feelin' his oats, or maybe he had a girl-friend on the side—who knows?—but he definitely was a better specimen than I had ever seen him be.

"How ya doin', kid?" Mickey said. "What's that outer-space monster alongside ya there?"

"That's Butkus, my large dog."

"Ya come over to show me your mutt?"

"Yo, Mick, can I have my locker back?"

"What's on your brain, kid?"

"Listen, how 'bout you whippin' me into shape, Mick?"

"Not me, kid, you wanna go blind?"

"The eye's great. What d'ya say, Mick? What d'ya think?"

"Every pug thinks they got one good one left. Look, kid, forget it, go home and forget it."

"Hey, we almost won, Mick. Mick, I done you a favor last time."

I guess what I said made some sense, 'cause Mickey stopped arguin' with me and moved closer to my face. He held up his finger alongside my left eye.

"Let's do a test . . . Tell me when you can see it," he said.

Mickey was movin' it forward and I seen it right away, so I said so.

"There's the little thing."

"That's real good. Now let's check the right lamp," Mickey said and held his finger next to my other eye, and I guess he started to move it forward. But I didn't see it. I didn't see nothin'. I had a feelin' he were still movin' it, but it was takin' twice as much time for me to see it. With my good eye I looked over at Mickey an' his face told me I was in trouble. I straightened my eyes back out just in time to see his finger sittin' almost in front of my face.

"I see it!"

"You see nothin'! Apollo Creed would flatten the side of your head with hooks. You ain't got the tools no more."

"Yeah," I said, and I was gettin' mad. "Maybe it's you who ain't got it no more!"

"Yeah, maybe you're right . . ." Mickey said in a quiet way and held his finger in front of his own nose. Then I seen this hand move, and suddenly he laid a roundhouse slap on the side of my face. ". . . but I don't think so. You didn't even see it comin' from a seventy-seven-year-old pug. What do you think the champ would do to ya, kid?"

"Hurt me bad."

"No, hurt ya permanent!"

"Hey, if I can't be fightin', maybe I can help around here. What d'ya think?"

"You want these guys watchin' you carry in towels and buckets?"

"I'm qualified . . . Mick, I just gotta be around it."

"Come by tomorrow."

21

APOLLO CREED WAS drumming his fingers on top of a beautifully ornate walnut desk. The desk itself, besides being surrounded by valuable artifacts and mementos, was also surrounded by several business associates.

Miles Jergens, Apollo's full-time promoter, seemed exasperated by having to argue with the champ over a moral question rather than a financial one. In other words, Apollo Creed was no longer speaking common sense, he was speaking emotionally, and that in Miles Jergens' book was bad business.

". . . I don't know about anyone else, but I want more pressure put on a rematch," Apollo Creed said.

"We're trying, but we received no response," Jergens said and lit a cigar.

"I think we ought to put our energies elsewhere," Apollo's lawyer added, but was not heard by either the promoter or the champion.

"Apollo, if we could command the same price

84

for two top contenders, then why pursue Balboa?"

"Jergens, maybe you don't understand this, but there are still a lot of people out there that think he won. Read my mail."

Apollo gestured back toward a rack of trophies that reached nearly to the ceiling. Beside the rack were three sacks of mail propped against the wall. Jergens tried for a mild smile and turned to the champion.

"Apollo, there are people out there whose opinions mean nothing."

"Not to me, with people accusin' me of havin' the fight fixed—callin' me a fake. My kids are bein' insulted at school."

"Apollo, there will be no rematch," Jergens said calmly.

"I don't wanna hear that!"

"Do you want to hear the truth? The last time he was damn lucky. Now he's finished. He's been idle for almost six months, and any good trainer would pass on him. Besides, this time you'd destroy him so badly the press would criticize you for fighting a has-been. Apollo, I say we go in another direction."

"I don't agree with that. I don't agree with any of it. Jergens, you're in charge of promotion; now listen up front, because I want a new campaign started, I want somethin' done publicly to bring this man out. Somethin' to jab his pride, somethin' to get the people around him talkin' . . . You get that goin' and I'll handle the rest."

"You're aware that if you use this humiliation tactic, you'll be setting yourself up as the bad guy," Jergens said and sighed.

"Whatever gets him in the ring."

22

MICKEY'S JOINT WAS filled with nearly fifty fighters in all colors and flavors. I tell ya, now that I wasn't poundin' a bag, now that I was just standin' there listenin' to it, the ropes snappin' against the floor, the speed bags, the heavy bags bein' dented with straight right hands, it all reminded me of kind of a crazy band with no conductor.

I was standin' near the wall holdin' this heavy bag for a young middleweight named Rick. Rick was maybe a guy like me who shoulda had somebody push him in another direction when he was young, but nobody was pushin' Rick, so he was gonna try his best to make it in the fight game. I hope he makes it, but I ain't so sure.

"Come on, Rick, get more hip into it," I said. "Keep your arm in tighter."

Rick was havin' trouble figurin' out what I was sayin', so I demonstrated it and snapped several sharp hooks into the bag.

"Lookin' good," Rick said.

At the next bag over, Mickey was workin' with

another middleweight. But he was havin' more problems than I was. Mickey was never one to keep his voice down when he was gettin' upset; the more mad he became inside, the more everyone around him was gonna hear about it.

"Come on, snap it in there—don't be so sloppy! Hey, Chico! I ain't talkin' to hear my head rattle! . . . Now, lemme tell you something else. Sometimes a good snarl can give you what the Bible calls a psychological edge. Now snarl and punch—snarl and punch!"

Chico, the middleweight, tried to snarl an' punch, but he kinda fell short of the mark and Mickey spit. I seen him turnin' his head in my direction and I had a feelin' I knew what was comin'.

"Yo, Rocky—come here!" Mickey yelled.

I walked over there and stood next to Chico, who looked kind of embarrassed. I rapped him once on the shoulder and he smiled.

"Show this Latin lamebrain how to snarl and punch," Mickey ordered.

"One snarling punch comin' up!" I turned around, set myself, an' snapped the bag with a hard right hook. I made such a mean snarl that I think I pulled a muscle in my upper lip. Mickey was very happy about the whole thing, and he laughed and stomped his foot on the floor.

"Now, that's ugly! That's snarlin'!" Mickey said, then he turned to me. "Okay, Rock, better get somebody to empty them buckets around the ring—they're spillin' over."

"I'll do it."

"No, let Mike do it."

"Come on, Mick, I don't mind."

And I didn't mind. I don't find it no disgrace to wrap my hand around the handle of a bucket and carry it into another room. I mean, somebody's gotta do the job, and since I wasn't runnin' for mayor, I was available. So I went over to the ring and took hold of this bucket full of spit. I had a feelin' somebody was watchin' me, and I looked up and I seen this guy named Chink Weber. Chink Weber, yeah, old Chink Weber was lookin' down on me. Chink Weber was some guy who had just come over from Jersey to try to make a name in Philly. He was a heavyweight who had a bad outlook on life. He hated everything, and for some reason he hated me the most.

"Hey, wait a minute!" Chink cried in a stale voice.

"Yeah?"

"I said wait a minute!"

I was about to wonder what Chink was tryin' to do, when he leaned over the top rope and spit down into the bucket, then gave me a very dirty look.

"Now you can take it," he said.

23

WHEN I WALKED across the street, it was dark and everybody was headin' home, and I seen Adrian workin' in the Pet Shop through that front window that they never clean. Yeah, she was cleanin' that five-gallon fish tank when I walked through the door and said, "How's everybody in the clubhouse tonight?"

"Fine. How'd your day go?"

"Fine, great—it's a nice job—clean fun, y'know. You need some help?"

"This water is heavy," Adrian said and handed me the bowl.

On the way over to pick up the bowl I almost tripped over Butkus layin' on the floor. Ol' Butkus was gettin' a little old, but he was still fun to have around.

"How ya doin', Butkus? Adrian, I was thinkin' maybe you oughta stay at the house and rest your stomach."

"The sixty dollars I make here part-time is gonna come in handy."

"Sure, but y'know what would really save money?"

"What?"

"Which of these fish do ya think is good to eat?" I said and smiled.

"Oh, Rocky," Adrian laughed back.

24

IT WAS KINDA cool that night as me and Adrian headed toward our house, but we was keepin' warm by jokin' around. I always liked jokin' around with Adrian, so here I was again, tellin' her some dumb story I learned maybe when I was in sixth grade.

". . . so I heard Two-Foot Maggie had an accident today."

"Who's Two-Foot Maggie?" Adrian asked.

"This girl I used to go with—y'know, when I was at school. And God give her this two-foot nose."

"Really?"

"Absolutely!"

"What kind of accident did she have?"

"Well, last night I heard she was sleepin', rolled over, got her nose caught in her ear, sneezed, and blew her brains out," I said.

"Oh, Rocky, that's terrible!"

"Yeah, it is pretty bad, isn't it?"

We were standin' in front of our house, and, as usual, the first thing I did was bend over and pick up about a half-dozen telegrams that were layin' there. I knew who they were from.

"I wish Apollo would leave you alone," Adrian said and picked up two telegrams before I could get to them.

"Yeah, he's spendin' a fortune on insults."

I unlocked the door an' we both went into the livin' room. For some reason the livin' room really looked empty. The television was sittin' on a crate, 'cause I couldn't afford to buy the table I wanted about a month ago. And this lamp I got on sale was sittin' on another crate. And the room itself, I hate to admit, was only half painted, and a pair of aluminum chairs were planted in front of the television. And the turtle bowl—I was hopin' by this time I'd have a good table for that—was also sittin' on a crate.

"I'd better start dinner—but I didn't have time to shop, Rocky," Adrian said.

"That's okay."

I watched Adrian move into the kitchen to start cookin', and I had to admit she was movin' different since she got pregnant. The whole sight kinda gave me a tickle inside. I was still thinkin' about Adrian when I heard a knock at the door and turned around and opened it. Before I knew it, this skinny guy with a scraggly beard shoved this white envelope into my stomach, yelled, "You've been served!" and ran away.

"Hey, come back here! What're you doin'?!" But the guy was running so fast he was outta sight before I knew it, an' I felt like a fool standin' out there on the curb yellin' down an empty street. I ran my finger inside the envelope and tore it open and took out a letter and read it underneath the light of a street lamp. I felt sick.

Adrian came to the door and looked out. "Rocky, what's the matter? What are you doing outside?"

"We lost it."

"Lost what?"

"The house."

25

THE NEXT DAY, or should I say the next morning, we wanted to get out of our house as fast as possible. I didn't wanna hang around and know that it didn't belong to us no more because I couldn't afford to pay for it, so we called Paulie, and here we was at his place.

Paulie was usin' Gazzo's car to haul over whatever stuff we had left, and Gazzo, I guess, was goin' along with the idea because he was sittin' in the front seat, even though he was sayin' nothin'.

"A couple more loads and we'll have this car empty," Paulie said.

"Yeah, hey, listen, Paulie, I appreciate this."

Gazzo finally turned around in the seat; he looked mad.

"Hey, I need you down on Ninth Street," he said to Paulie.

"I'll meet ya down there."

"I need ya now," Gazzo said in a firm way.

"I'll meet ya there—you don't need me **holdin'** your hand."

Gazzo gave Paulie a hard look and drove off, and Paulie turned to me and smiled.

"Family comes first, y'know. Let me tell you about the history of banks. Banks have no sense of friggin' humor—listen, when things look like they can't get no worse, don't worry, they will," Paulie said and punched my arm.

I nodded and took the last of some pots and pans and handed Paulie the turtle bowl, which was covered with tinfoil.

"When you gonna donate these things to science?" Paulie said.

"Who? Cuff and Link? Come on, they're my friends."

"That's your problem . . . I remember when we used to flatten a few of these creeps thumbin' to the shore every summer!"

Before I could say anything in defense of my turtles, we were walkin' through the front door, and I couldn't believe what I seen. I guess since Adrian had moved out, nothin' had been cleaned, 'cause hundreds of beer cans was everywhere an' maybe two hundred pounds of clothes was hangin' from everythin'. I seen a brick was thrown into the television, an' there were about five holes punched in the wall. Over on the table were a couple hundred TV-dinner foil plates stacked. I'd estimate the place was a mess.

"Nice place, Paulie."

"Forget what you see. Everythin's under control —nobody got hurt here."

"Y'know, I feel very disgraced by this," I said.

"You mean disgraced by my house here?"

"No, about havin' to move in and everythin'."

"Come on, everybody goes through rough periods . . . There's times when creeps don't pay up for weeks and I gotta apply outside pressure," Paulie said and imitated like he was stranglin' somebody.

"Y'oughta quit that job."

"I been makin' some big connections in New York—big-time. Bein' Gazzo's flunky ain't for me . . . Rock, don't blame yourself for losing everythin', 'cause what you gone through I don't think I coulda handled it without breakin' some heads. Hey, the crapper's over there," Paulie said and pointed.

We was walkin' down the only hallway in the apartment, and I seen the door at the end was opened a little and Adrian was sittin' on the side of the bed, just staring into nothingness. Paulie stuck his big head into the room and talked loud. "Hey, for somebody who's gettin' free room an' board, you don't look too happy, Adrian!"

"Thank you, Paulie," Adrian said softly.

"Sure, and don't feel like you owe me nothin' either. It's nothin', really. I don't mind doin' charity."

"Paulie, how 'bout we see ya later?" I said.

"Sure, but don't try to run the sink an' flush at the same time—it's no good. Hey, everythin's gonna be good for youse, I know about these things," Paulie said and left.

I was glad that Paulie stepped outta the room, 'cause I could see he was havin' a bad effect on his sister. I walked in and touched Adrian's beautiful shiny brown hair and said, "I'm sorry for the inconvenience."

"You don't have to apologize for anything."

"I'm still sorry."

26

BOY, THE GYM was poundin' with life as usual, and
that's the way I liked it. I know I coulda gotten a
lotta other jobs if I really wanted to, but there was
somethin' about the gym that I liked, and it was
impossible for me to stay away from it. At the
moment I was holdin' this heavy bag for a middleweight as he pounded away. I was tryin' to concentrate on the way the middleweight was hookin' his
left into the bag, but I couldn't keep my eye from
wanderin' over to Chink, that heavyweight with the
bad temper, and several of his pals who were lookin'
at a newspaper and laughin' . . . They were still
laughin' when they all started to move toward me.

"Where's your heart?" Chink yelled out.

Heart? I didn't know what he was talkin' about.
And before I could ask that question, one of Chink's
friends held out a newspaper for me to look at.

"No stones—you're givin' boxin' a bad name."

I still didn't know what he was talkin' about 'til
I seen this here full-page ad right in front of me,
of Apollo Creed pluckin' a cartoon drawin' of a

chicken with my head attached. Mickey come over and snatched the newspaper away.

"Let me see that!" Mickey said.

I knew Mickey was gonna say somethin' and try to defend me, but I didn't wanna hear it. I couldn't believe what Creed was tryin' to do to get me back in the ring. I wouldn't mind gettin' back in the ring, but I had made a promise, an' this was the way I guessed I was gonna have to pay for it. I was movin' toward the door when I bumped into Chink's manager.

"Oops!"

"Couldn't you think of anythin' tougher to say than 'oops'?" Chink's manager said and laughed.

"You got no stones," Chink yelled.

Everyone laughed as I moved away, and the last thing I could hear was Mickey's voice echoing down the hall.

"The next one who rides him can get the hell out!"

27

I GUESS THERE were about eight guys hangin' out at the bar at Andy's as Andy was crackin' some eggs into a glass. I was a little drunk, but I had to admit I was enjoyin' the attention an' tryin' to shoot pool with this other guy. He was more drunk than I was, so I think if this game were left uninterrupted, it would most likely go on until we was in our nineties.

"How many's that?" Andy asked and broke another egg.

". . . seven!" a guy I didn't know said.

"Go for ten—let's go for ten!" Andy asked.

"I got five bucks that says you throw up," another guy I didn't know said.

"I'll cover that. Who else wants to bet?" I yelled, but didn't know why I was betting. I didn't have five cents in my pocket.

"I'll bet ya ten more, Rock," Andy said and handed me this tall glass with ten raw eggs in it. "Matter of fact, I'll bet ya twenty more you can't go for it, Rock." Andy made a sick face.

"C'mon, gimme the glass."

Andy handed me the glass an' I held it up to the light so everyone could get a good look at it, then I brought it toward my mouth.

"First ya relax—then you think of wet candy—" I said and started to drink. They watched the ten yokes slide down my throat, an' soon they all disappeared and I was laughin' inside because almost everyone was sick. I didn't have to ask for the wager money, it was all layin' on the bar. I think everyone was glad to pay an' get away.

"It's no problem, it all goes down in one string," I said. I was just foldin' the money to put in my pocket when I seen Paulie enter, and he come over and tapped my shoulder.

"Ever think about takin' that act to Vegas?" Paulie said in a dry voice. "Yeah, it's a real thriller, Rock! How 'bout you and me go talk?" Before I could say anything, Paulie had his hand under my elbow and we was walkin' toward the men's room.

The men's room, as usual, was revoltin' even for me, who was feelin' kinda revoltin' myself. Paulie walked about three feet in front of me, turned around, and said, "How's your brain, Rock?"

"Fine, how's your brain?"

"My brain's better than your brain 'cause at least I know what's happenin' around ya."

"I know what's happenin' around me."

"You know nothin', 'cause if you did you wouldn't be playin' no fool for these bums!" Paulie said, and I could tell he was gettin' mad.

"I ain't no fool."

"Don't gimme no lip, Rock, I'm on top of this—no lip. Hey, I'm embarrassed for ya. I see you drinkin' friggin' eggs—and I'm embarrassed for ya!"

"I'm embarrassed, too, y'know. What am I supposed to do about it?"

"Look, Adrian asked ya not to take no more beatin's. I don't respect that. I think you should do what you want! But if she wants to keep ya alive, that's nice. Ya don't wanna mix with Creed no more, that's nice, too. In my eyes here, ya nailed 'im, you got nothin' to prove to nobody . . . So don't be no chump, don't ever be puttin' yourself down on none of these bums' levels!" Paulie kinda smacked my cheek and I laughed.

"When did you get so smart?"

"I ain't so smart, you're just dumber than I am," Paulie said and laughed. Now that Paulie had gotten all this stuff off his chest, he was feelin' like a kid again an' jabbed at me an' I jabbed back an' was feelin' pretty good inside. "Let's get outta here," Paulie said.

We wasn't halfway through the door when Andy yelled from behind the bar, "Yo, Rock, fifty says you can't do ten more eggs!"

I knew I could do ten more, but the point was I didn't wanna do no more.

"That's beneath my level, Andy."

Paulie laughed, and me and him stepped outta Andy's joint and into the night air.

28

I WALKED INTO Paulie's place, which had now become like a boardinghouse to me, and I seen Adrian in the kitchen whippin' up some dinner. I walked past the television set and seen that the news was on, but since I wasn't in the mood to hear any bad news, I just drifted into the kitchen.

"Workin' late? Is everything all right, Rocky?"

"Absolutely."

"Are you hungry?"

"I already ate at the office."

"I missed you today," Adrian said and started to bend over and put away some cleanser. I seen her face suddenly get red and she tensed over in pain.

I ran over to her. "You all right? Come on, sit down. You all right?" Adrian didn't say nothin' and I guided her to the couch.

"Ahhhh." She took a deep breath and held up her hand like she was wavin' away the pain. "I'm all right—really."

Adrian settled back in the chair an' took several deep breaths. I was a little scared 'cause I had never seen her do this, so I kept holdin' her hand. Then I got mad 'cause I was thinkin' maybe this was happenin' because she was workin' part-time to help support this family.

"That's it, you can't work no more," I said.

"Believe me, Rocky, I feel all right . . . I'm just tired."

I wasn't sure if I was gonna believe her or if she was just tryin' to be proud and not let me know how much she was hurtin' inside. I was still thinkin' about all these things when I looked at the television just as Apollo Creed was bein' interviewed by some announcer.

". . . and today Howard spoke with Apollo Creed, and, as usual, Creed was not at a loss for words."

Apollo was lookin' straight at the camera, and his eyes seemed to be jumpin' outta the screen. He seemed very serious and very mad for some reason when he talked.

"I know a lotta people wanted to see me in a rematch with a timid fellow named the Italian Scallion, but the man does not have the honor to meet me in the ring. Why I do not know, but I do know this is Apollo Creed sayin' that if Rocky Balboa fights me, there won't be enough left of him to bounce off a wall!"

Mickey was lying in his dumpy room watching the same television broadcast. He was listening while gazing at his big toe inching its way through a hole in a gray wool sock.

". . . my plans were to entertain the American public by having this be a classic rematch—a special match to prove this lucky club fighter cannot last five minutes with a superior athlete like me!"

I couldn't believe Apollo Creed was sayin' all this stuff about me, because I thought we had a

good friendship goin'. I respected who he was an'
I thought maybe he would respect who I was, but
for some reason he was really gettin' down on me.

"... so to you, Italian Stallion, I dedicate this
poem ...

> You may not be the brightest,
> But the time is surely the rightest,
> So Lord let him see the glorious light
> And give him enough guts to fight."

Apollo finished talking, and the announcer looked
very serious and shook hands with the champion.

"Thank you for your candidness, Apollo."

I didn't wanna hear no more, so I just walked
away and went to the bedroom and closed the door.
I was standin' in front of the dressing mirror, lookin'
closely at my face an' wonderin' why all this bad
luck was comin' my way. I never done nobody no
wrong and now I was gettin' it from all sides. I was
still feelin' sorry for myself when Adrian walked in
and come up to me.

"Y'know, I used to be a fighter, not so good, but
if somebody was to say, 'Whaddaya do for a livin'?'
I could say, 'Yo, I throw my hands for a livin'.'
Now I can't say nothin' ... Adrian, y'know, I'm
gettin' very weary 'cause I think I'm becomin' a
nobody forever."

"In whose eyes? Not mine."

"In mine," I said and tapped my head. "In here."

"You gave me your word, Rocky."

"That was before we got hungry and we was
thrown outta our house!"

"Paulie would've lent us some money."

"I don't wanna borrow from nobody. I don't like
livin' here either! I can earn my own livin'. Adrian,

y'know, it's like I don't wanna do no other jobs, 'cause deep down inside I don't think I've gone all the way I can as a fighter. I still think I got some good stuff left in me."

"Rocky, if I can take it, why can't you?" Adrian's voice was gettin' angry. "Am I stronger than you? No, you don't see or hear me complaining, so why don't you stop making up all these excuses for wanting to go backwards?"

"Boxin's my life!"

"It *was* your life."

"Please, I didn't ask you to stop bein' a woman, so don't ask me to stop bein' a man— I'm sorry."

I heard a knock at the door an' that made me feel good, 'cause I didn't wanna argue with Adrian no more. Adrian was the last person in the world I wanted to fight. I kissed her and went to the door.

When I walked away from Adrian, I felt like I had been sayin' the right thing, 'cause I was a fighter and I did have a few other things to prove to myself, so why shouldn't I? I was still thinkin' about that when I opened the front door and looked out and seen Mickey staring at me.

"I think we should knock his block off!" Mickey yelled.

"Absolutely," I said.

29

ME AND APOLLO were sittin' in the Pennsylvania Boxing Commission office, and in front of us was a long table surrounded by reporters and photographers and a lot of film crews and what looked like a whole forestful of microphones. I was feelin' nervous; I was glad Mickey was sittin' beside me, and Paulie was observin' from the other side of the room. I looked over as Apollo's trainer was wipin' the sweat from his head and eyin' me. Apollo looked kinda mad and wasn't his usual jokin'-around self. I mean, the stuff he was sayin' was kinda funny, but he wasn't sayin' it in a funny way, if you know what I mean.

"Apollo, where will this fight be held?" a reporter asked.

"Philadelphia," Apollo answered.

"Why Philly again?" another reporter asked.

"Because I want all his hometown people there to see him get the beatin' of his life."

"Rocky, do you have any predictions?" a reporter asked me.

"No, none that I can think of."

Apollo leaned over to me and looked me right in the eye and said, "Italian Scallion, I come here special from my modern training camp, where I been breathin' clean air and gettin' very strong, to tell you to be very smart and after this fight donate what's gonna be left of your body to science . . . So beware, man."

I gotta admit, if Apollo was tryin' to get me nervous, he was doin' great.

"Rocky, your share of the gate is nearly a million dollars. What're you gonna do with it?" a reporter asked.

"Well, first I'm gonna get some new hats, mebbe a motorcycle, a coupla quarts of perfume for Adrian, a statue for the church, all the Muppet toys for the new kid, an' mebbe a snow-cone machine for Paulie, he likes snow cones."

Apollo turned to the cameras and held up his fist. "The man's crazy."

"Apollo, there have been many people who believe you lost the first fight. Care to comment?"

"The last time I was out there, I was outta shape and he was lucky. This time you'll see the real Apollo Creed."

"Do you feel this time you have a chance against Apollo?" a reporter asked me.

"I dunno, he looks pretty mad."

"He'll punch his heart out!" Paulie yelled from the other side of the room.

Everybody turned and looked at Paulie, but he didn't care. He pointed at Apollo Creed an' spoke even louder than he done a coupla seconds before.

"The Rock will drop 'im like a bad habit," Paulie said.

"Who's that, Al Capone?" Apollo said and sneered at Paulie.

"Now, some of you people may not like me, but you gotta admit Apollo Creed is one damn ingenious, one hundred percent pure, Afro-American folk hero, and this October he will provide the ultimate gala spectacle! Be there, because October first I'm gonna unleash the most feared weapon ever devised since the atom bomb. October first you're gonna meet head-on with the most paralyzing punch you've ever seen, Italian Stallion, so beware!" the champion said and sat back down in his seat.

"Rocky, do you have anything derogatory to say about the champion?" a voice asked me.

"Yeah, he's great."

"How about some clowning shots, Apollo?" a reporter asked.

Apollo looked right at the reporter and said, "Clowning shots—does this look like some kind of a circus?" Apollo took one last dry look at me. "You're all mine!" he said an' walked outta the room an' left all the reporters hangin' there with their jaws open.

I turned to Mickey. "He's still upset," I said.

The following mornin' was kinda cold for a summer mornin', and me and Mickey was standin' outside this gymnasium. Me, I was dressed in the same old worn-out sweatsuit that I always wore, because I had become kinda superstitious about it. I held the door for Mickey as he drug out this old bicycle and banged it once on the cement to kinda shake off all the spiders that had been livin' between the spokes; then he got on the old thing.

"It's time to do some roadwork—hey, kid, you gotta wear that rotten sweatsuit?"

"It's an original," I said.

"It smells up the neighborhood."

"It brings me luck."

"It brings ya flies! Now, let's get some blood back in them legs—come on, let's go!"

Apollo was sparring in his mountain-lodge gymnasium with an opponent who somewhat resembled Rocky and his boxing style. The sparring partner was crouched low and hooking left and hooking right and doing the best he could to reach Apollo's body with his ever-moving fists. Apollo feinted with his left and dropped his sparring partner with three straight right hands in a row.

"Get me another one," Apollo said.

It was still just about midmornin' when me and Mickey were watchin' some 8mm films of my fight with Apollo. We was runnin' it in Mickey's office, which was kinda hot and small, but it was the only place that had a movie screen. Well, not really a movie screen. Mickey had nailed his top sheet up on the wall and we was watchin' it on the wrinkled thing.

"See the way he moves . . . he can cold-cock ya with either hand—he's the best—you gotta have a lot a guts to go in there again, Rock."

"Thanks."

"But left-handed fighters are the worst, always waitin' to throw one big punch! No class in southpaws."

"Why didn't you tell me this before?"

"Didn't wanna hurt ya' feelin's—see how clumsy ya are? See how your clumsy style confuses him not much, but enough? What I figure is, you gotta develop speed. You have to do a lotta leanin' and a lotta jabbin' and keep him from knockin' ya' bad eye out—ya gotta learn to fight right-handed."

"I can't change now."

"There ain't no can'ts; ya gotta, understand?"

"He don't do nothin' wrong," I said.

Mickey coughed and stood in front of the projector, and I watched all these images of me and Apollo flashin' across his chest.

"Sure he does—he's fightin' us again, ain't he?!"

Apollo Creed was working himself into a lather as he danced around his second sparring partner of the day. This sparring partner was having less luck with him than the first one and was receiving a volley of machine-gun rights and lefts into his face, and in a few short moments was lying semi-conscious on the canvas.

Apollo's trainer stepped in and toweled the champion down.

"You better slow down, champ."

"Get me another one," Apollo said.

Mickey drug me over to the YMCA, and there I was standin' up to my waist in water, swingin' this thirty-pound dumbbell under the water. I wasn't feelin' very enthusiastic about it, because I didn't know how much sense it made, but Mickey was tellin' me Marciano used to do this to build up some punchin' power, so who was I to complain? Plus, learnin' to be a right-handed fighter was gettin' to be harder than I thought. But the thing that'd been botherin' me was Adrian still not goin' along with this fightin' idea and makin' my life kinda difficult, so I'd asked Paulie to come over and we was talkin' about it.

"So whaddaya want me to do?" Paulie asked.

"Talk to her," I said and pumped a dumbbell. "Last night Adrian started cryin'. She don't like this."

"Shut up and concentrate!" Mickey yelled. "That's it, stretch and swing till it hurts! . . . Stretch! Get angry, get mad, don't drown, and do it five hundred more times."

Apollo's face was contorted every time he received the medicine ball in his midsection. His trainer had one of the larger sparring partners at the gym firing the ball into the champion's stomach with all his force, and Apollo took it without a sound of pain. The champion appeared to be in another world.

Little Mike was throwin' this medicine ball into my stomach, and usually it never hurt before, but tonight it was hurtin'. I think it was hurtin' because I weren't concentratin' on what I was doin'. I was thinkin' more about Adrian an' how she was feelin' than how I was feelin' at this moment. I felt bad for Mickey because he was sittin' there tryin' to coach me on, but I just couldn't concentrate on what I was doin', y'know.

"I told you this once before, and I'm tellin' ya again—we waited a long time for this—we came close! We shoulda won, but this time you're gonna be scary—this time you're gonna be a greasy monster! Come on, pay attention!" Mickey yelled.

". . . I think I've had it, Mick," I said and walked toward the locker room.

Apollo was pounding away at the heavy bag in his deserted gym. The whole room had an eerie feeling about it as the heavy bag's shadow extended up and down the wall, somewhat resembling a lynched body. The champion threw punch after punch into the heavy bag until it appeared it would nearly come off its chain.

Mickey had me workin' the heavy bag, an' again I weren't feelin' so hot. Usually the heavy bag was my best exercise. I seen in the background Paulie was watchin' and puffin' on a cigar while sittin' on the bleachers. Mickey was still yellin' at me like a coach. "This time I'm gonna pound that olive oil outta ya, and this time you're gonna be so mean, you're gonna chew razors. So mean you're gonna spit nails and eat fire! Ya' gonna bob an' weave an' pound an' get pounded—"

"Let's take a break, Mick."

"You better get this woman off your mind—you better get your mind straight!" Mickey yelled.

I shrugged and didn't know what to say, an' watched as Paulie threw his cigar down and left.

The next day I was sparrin' with this shifty lightweight, tryin' to get some speed in my movements, but I felt dead.

"Speed—speed!" Mickey yelled. "This time they're gonna have to keep ya in a cage . . . 'cause this time ya' gonna be a greasy, fast, two-hundred-pound Italian tank that ain't gonna be stopped!! C'mon, catch that little guy—cut the ring off—c'mon, ya look dead out there! Ya can catch that speedball, ya can catch Creed easy—"

I shot a look at Mickey an' he looked mad, an' behind him I seen Paulie standin'.

"Time!" Mickey yelled. "What the hell's the matter with you?!"

"Nothin'."

"I wanna tell ya somethin'. For a forty-five-minute fight, ya gotta train forty-five thousand minutes—that's right—forty-five thousand—ten weeks. You ain't even trained one!"

I couldn't think of nothin' to say, an' Mickey just walked away.

"Yo, Rock," Paulie said.

"Yo, Paulie?"

"Yo, Rock . . . I'm worried about ya."

"Why?"

"Ya' head ain't on right—I been watchin'!"

"Hey, listen, I'm doin' all right. Hey, ya wanna help work my corner, ya wanna get involved in this fight?"

"Involved in what? Watchin' ya get murdered?"

"I'll be okay," I said, but weren't so sure.

"C'mon!" Paulie yelled. "My sister's got ya feelin' so guilty for fightin', ya don't know if ya' comin' or goin'! It ain't right, what she's doin'!"

"It's all right."

"No, it ain't right!"

"Yo, Paulie, forget it. Adrian's okay—forget it," I said an' seen Paulie was on his way out.

I was climbin' outta the ring when Mickey come over lookin' real mad-like.

"I liked ya better when ya was emptyin' spit buckets!"

"What's that mean?"

"It means ya' trainin' like a ninth-rate pug who oughta be pumpin' gas in Jersey!"

"I think I'm gonna go take a shower," I said an' knew Mickey was right.

"Yo, Adrian, where the hell are you?!" Paulie said as he entered the Pet Shop.

Adrian looked up from the birdseed she was presently stacking.

"Paulie?"

"Yeah, Paulie. What the hell's goin' on with you?!"

"What do you mean?"

"Answer me. What the hell's goin' on?"

Adrian backed up. "About what, Paulie?"

"About what ya' doin' to that guy over there."

"Please don't start, Paulie. I'm doing what I have to do to keep him safe."

Paulie grabbed the birdseed rack and flung it against the wall.

"This is how I brought ya up, to ditch this guy when he needs ya helpin' out? I don't believe my ears!"

"You never taught me anything—and you don't know what you're talking about!"

"Don't tell me! He's gonna get hurt bad because of you!"

"Don't say that!"

"I'm sayin' it!"

"If he gets hurt," Adrian said, starting to cry, "if he gets hurt, you won't have to live with it. I will."

Paulie paid no attention to his sister's argument and grabbed her arm. "Go over there an' tell him it's all right!"

Adrian exploded. "No, it's not all right! If he goes blind, you can walk away from it, but I can't! It's not all right, it's not! I love him, you don't!!"

Adrian felt the pain start deep in her abdomen and shoot straight to her head. She fell against Paulie.

I was still gettin' dressed an' thinkin' it weren't

such a good day so far when Mickey come in, an'
he still looked mad . . . maybe madder.

"C'mon."

"C'mon what?" I said.

"C'mon, where's ya' guts?"

"What's ya' problem, Mick?"

"I ain't the problem, you're the one who ain't got
the heart no more—let's see ya' guts! Don't ya got
nothin' inside no more? Ya' trainin' like a damn
bum!"

I hated that word.

"Bum?"

"Yeah, bum."

"Maybe ya' right—maybe I ain't got it no more."

"Then don't waste my time, ya bum!" Mickey
screamed louder than I ever heard. "Go back to the
docks where ya belong! Go back to bein' a two-bit
nothin'! 'Cause I'm too old to waste my time trainin'
a loser, you bum! ! !"

He made me feel so bad I wanted to smash my
fists into the locker until they was just bloody,
broken things.

Johnny come runnin' in.

"Rock, they want ya across the street!"

"What's the matter?"

"Ya' wife's sick!"

My legs, my damn legs, wouldn't move no faster.
I wanted to move my legs so fast that they would
catch fire an' melt the street. I wanted to be in that
Pet Shop in one split second, an' I was tryin'. I run
down the steps of Mickey's gym an' hit that front
door as hard as I could; I didn't care if there was a
lock on it or nothin'. If it was locked I was gonna
bust right through it, but luckily it was open and the
door swung wide and I was standin' in the street. I

didn't see if there was any traffic, 'cause I didn't care. I hit the sidewalk in front of the Pet Shop and went runnin' right inside. For a second I froze in the doorway 'cause I couldn't understand what was happenin'—I mean, when you walked into a place a thousand times before an' you seen it one way, like with Adrian standin' behind the cash register or cleanin' the bird cage or somethin' like that, but now I walked in and it was a whole different picture. There was my wife layin' on the floor with her brother cradlin' her head in his lap.

I felt sick. I dropped down, kissed her, an' stroked her hair.

"What happened?" I said to Paulie.

"Nothin'. We was just talkin' loud and she dropped down. I don't know what happened!"

"Adrian, how bad is it?" I said to her, but I didn't hear nothin' comin' back. She moved her head a little, like she was tryin' to talk, but she didn't have the strength to say anythin'. And now I was gettin' scared.

"Did you call the ambulance?" I said to Paulie.

"On the way."

I leaned down and kissed Adrian's cheek and said —and I believed this, too—"Adrian, it's gonna be okay—it's gonna be okay . . ."

30

THAT SMELL WAS in my nose again.

The smell that comes with hospitals. I don't know if it's the paint, I don't know if it's the knockout drops, I don't know what it is, I don't know if it's the smell of sickness, but in every hospital there's that smell, and here I was again, but I wished it was me who was in the hospital. I wished it weren't Adrian, I wished it were me. I think I coulda taken it. I didn't know if she could take it. I had been in and out of hospitals all my life, a stitch here, a stitch there, a broken bone here an' a broken bone there. So it didn't make no difference to me. But Adrian was different, she wasn't used to pain. At least not the kind of pain that I thought she was in, so I was gettin' very worried. I almost asked Paulie for a cigarette, but I knew that wasn't gonna help matters, an' there was enough smell an' stink in the hospital without me addin' to it, y'know what I mean?

I was thinkin' all kinds of stupid thoughts about what had happened. If it were me who'd caused it, or whether Paulie had caused it, an' if Paulie did cause it, I swear to God I was gonna . . . nah, forget that, that ain't gonna help nothin', 'cause if I started thinkin' along those lines, in five minutes I would jump all over Paulie an' I wouldn't even know if he was guilty of nothin'. He had always argued with his sister, so I couldn't go punchin' him now and expect that it would change anything. I was rubbin' my eyes when I looked up an' I seen the doctor come out. He come right over to us.

"Mr. Balboa?" the doctor said.

"Right here."

"The baby is fine, even though it's a month premature."

"What is it?" Paulie asked.

"A boy."

A boy. A real boy.

Not a rubber doll.

Not a cartoon.

A real boy.

I couldn't believe it. In one year my life was changed so much. Now I had a son. I turned to Paulie and said, "How 'bout you say congratulations?"

"Congratulations! . . . I can't believe my sister done it!"

"Where's Adrian?" I asked the doctor. "How's Adrian?"

"She's had complications."

I knew it. I knew everythin' was going too good to be true. Now I felt that sick feelin' in my stomach again. I could feel my fist curlin' an' uncurlin', and I didn't know what to say, because if he told me something bad, I was gonna look for the nearest window an' jump outta it. Now I was talkin' stupid again. If anything was wrong, Adrian needed me

here an' that's where I would be, but I was feelin'
very mixed up right then.

"Like what?"

"Your wife was hemorrhaging when she was
brought in. The premature delivery was most likely
caused by straining, and the sudden loss of blood
has made her slip into a coma . . ."

I walked into the room where Adrian was lyin',
an' it was dark. I was movin' toward Adrian's bed
when my eyes started to hurt an' get red. She
looked like she was sleepin', but I knew she was in
bad trouble. I come very close to Adrian and I
kissed her.

"Adrian, yo, Adrian, it's me, Rocky . . . They
says you're in a coma—I don't wanna believe that.
I wanna believe you're tired and you're doin' some
deep sleepin'—so don't worry about nothin'. You
sleep as long as you want 'cause I'm gonna be here
when you wake up."

The door opened and I looked up and I seen
Paulie walk inside real quiet-like. I could see he
was standin' straight and tryin' to be strong, but he
was feelin' the same way I was doin'.

"Rock . . ." Paulie said to me, "there's nothin'
you can do here. Let's go see the kid. This is what
my sister would want you to do."

"We gotta see him together."

It was a coupla hours later when the door to
Adrian's room opened and I heard the sound of a
nurse's shoes comin' close to me. I kept lookin' at
Adrian an' down at the book I was readin' to her.
It wasn't that good of a book, I think it was a
western, 'bout some guys trapped in a gulch in a
cross fire and battlin' their way out. Paulie had

been sittin' in the chair for the past couple of hours, just rubbin' his head and shakin' it back and forth.

" '. . . Jim made a pack with his other belongings . . . what to do? How to get outta here with all these guns blazin' around me, he thought,' " I said and turned the page. The nurse's shoes stopped behind me, an' I knew what words she was gonna say to me.

"Mr. Balboa, visiting hours are over," she said.

"Can't I stay? I'll be quiet."

"I'm sorry, those are hospital rules. You'll have to leave now."

I was about to ask the nurse another question, like maybe if she covered me with a sheet, if I stood behind the curtain, or if she faked some kind of pass, could I stay there, when Paulie stood up and looked at me. He was cryin'.

"I can't do this no more—I can't do this, watchin' her like this," Paulie said and walked outta the room.

I felt very bad for Paulie, because as much as he used to fight with his sister all the time and call her names, I knew deep down inside this was his way of showin' love. Paulie was one of them kind of people that couldn't say love, he had to say other words to describe love, like insults. As long as he kept insultin' you, that meant he liked you.

It was twisted.

It was unusual.

But it was Paulie.

"Do ya have a chapel?"

Paulie wasted no time in going to the nurses' desk. His face was flushed and he appeared to be quite distraught as he confronted what appeared to be the head nurse.

"Who's in charge around here?"

"Dr. Boyd," the nurse said.

"And where is he? C'mon, where is he? I'm standin' here waitin' for an answer."

"In the lounge—it's over there."

Paulie turned away from the nurses' desk and started across the hallway, almost trampling an intern who was carrying what appeared to be a rack of specimen bottles. Following the nurse's directions, he entered a small room marked PHYSICIANS' LOUNGE and saw three men in white jackets sitting around drinking coffee with an attractive nurse.

"I'm lookin' for Boyd."

"Can I help you?"

"Yeah, I wanna tell you somethin'. My sister's lyin' sick in your hospital. If somethin' happens to her because you guys didn't do the right thing, you better know I'm comin' for ya."

I was so nervous standin' there lookin' through this glass window watchin' the nurse move along a row of sleepin' babies. A lot of people say that babies all look the same, but I don't agree. Every face I seen had a different kind of look, y'know, attitude, like they was thinkin' about somethin' inside, and even though they couldn't put it into the English language, it was comin' out on their faces. Some faces were kind of curled up, and others were really smooth and relaxed, and others kind of in between. I don't know if it really has anything to do with life in general, but it seemed like they all had different attitudes even at that age.

The nurse kept movin' along, and she stopped in front of a sleepin' baby. I couldn't believe this was my kid. I couldn't believe it for a second. I couldn't believe that little thing lyin' there so peaceful, not knowing what's goin' on, was my kid. He was a winner. He was definitely a leadin' man. His face looked so relaxed, and his nose was kinda turned up like his mother's, and already he had dark hair; oh, yeah, this kid didn't resemble me hardly at all, which meant he was off to a pretty good start. I don't know why my stupid eyes started to get red, but I could feel them burnin'. There was no smog in the hospital, there was no other reason, except somethin' inside was makin' me do this, a feeling I'd never experienced before, y'know? I was a father. This had really happened, and I could look forward to this kid bein' a million times better than I was. Better in school, better in stickball; he could sure be better dressed than me; oh, yeah, just kidding. I tapped on the window and tried to figure out something to say. I wanted the first words that I said to my son to be important, but I knew they would be okay, y'know, like almost important. I would think of all the important things an hour later. That always happened, but I tried anyway.

". . . I'm your father," I was whispering. "I don't know your name yet, 'cause Adrian didn't tell me nothin' yet . . . but listen, don't you worry about nothin', 'cause everything's gonna be okay. What's happened here is just a little postponement, y'know. Things like this happen, 'cause some people were just born to be tested all the time. I'm always bein' tested, things never turn out all the way bad, y'know, but I'm always bein' tested, so don't worry about nothin', 'cause we're gonna pass this test, you and me, and everything's gonna be okay."

31

THE CHAPEL WAS very small an' the altar was small an' the ceiling weren't high either, not like the chapels we have back in the old neighborhood, which were old chapels. But a chapel's a chapel when ya need to pray and talk private, y'know. I was thinkin' about blessin's in general. I was thinkin' about how some people get all the breaks an' go through life without skinnin' their knees, an' how other people get beat up by the city life, y'know, at every turn; that life ain't nothin' but a war. And I don't know who has it better off, who can say at the age of maybe sixty-five or eighty that, yeah, I lived a full life. Probably the guy who had done all the battlin'. I know I been scrappin' and fightin' ever since I was old enough to know what pain felt like, an' I ain't stopped. But I always believed that if you lowered your head an' went full steam ahead, you had to at least win, or almost win. The very worst you could do was come in a good second. Right now I was lowerin' my head and prayin' as hard as I could for my wife.

I seen Mickey walk in.

He walked until he was almost in front of the altar, an' just stared at me for a couple of minutes.

"Rocky . . . it's three in the morning . . ."

I didn't really care what time it was. Besides, what difference did it make? I was stayin' there no matter what.

"I went to ya' house, they told me you was here— it's three in the morning, kid."

"Yeah."

"Look, kid . . . I'm very sorry about what happened here. Adrian's a good girl, and me, I'm sorry for ya both, I am . . . but I gotta tell ya somethin' else one time, then I ain't sayin' it again. You're gettin' another shot at the greatest title in the world. You're gonna be swappin' shots with the greatest fighter in the world . . . in the Garden! . . . In case your mind's been slippin', all this happens pretty soon."

Mickey walked back and forth in front of the altar.

"We gotta get you to that good trainin'. Time's short! Look, Rock, what you had happen is bad an' terrible, but there ain't nothin' you can do about it here. This shot is probably our last shot, and if you think I'm gonna sit here while everything we broke our horns for, everything we've busted our lives for, is gonna get away from us, you're nuts! ! ! I didn't wanna get mad in a Biblical place like this, but I'm gettin' mad!"

Mickey was almost mad enough to curse, but I didn't think he had enough nerve to do it in a chapel, an' he didn't, but he started walkin' toward me and I seen an expression in his face I never seen before. He was scared; he was scared for us both.

"Lemme give you some facts of life. Ya' equipment ain't the best, for openers. You ain't in the best of shape either! Ya lean too far forward, ya drag your back foot, ya carry your left low—there's twenty guys who should be able to mop the canvas with you. All you got is a hook and a hard head, that's it! So you can't lay down like this on yourself, you gotta train, or we're gonna get killed!" Mickey slapped the side of the bench hard. "I don't know how to get through your thick head, but there's a very tough fighter out there lookin' to break your face and show everybody you're nothin' but a bum who got lucky! I didn't wanna get mad. But now you got me mad, 'cause what you're doin' is wrong! So you better understand that without you I'm nothin' but an old man with a loud voice, and without me you're just a has-been who's emptyin' spit buckets. So if we blow this shot, damn it, we're gonna blow it together, 'cause if you're stayin', I'm stayin'!"

The light that came through Adrian's window was just bright enough for me to see the pages of this book I was readin' to her. I was holdin' this western book that I was readin' to her the night before in one hand, and I was holdin' Adrian's hand in my free hand. Mickey, he was sittin' in the corner rubbin' his eyes an' hopin' everythin' would come out good very soon.

" '. . . From his lookout post he looked at the outlaws who were about to fire at the sheriff. Louie got out his rifle and aimed at the leader . . .' " I said and read.

Paulie stood in the hallway with flowers in his hands. He tried to enter Adrian's room perhaps a half dozen times but somehow failed to get up enough nerve to enter. The sight of his sister in her unconscious state depressed him so much that on his final attempt to enter the room he stopped, dropped the flowers in the hallway, and leaned against the wall, shaking his head in disbelief.

It was nighttime and I was havin' a lotta trouble readin'. But that was the least of my problems cause I had to stay with Adrian as long as they would allow me to stay here, and I was gonna do just that. I figured if I kept talkin' to her, kept what-do-ya-call it, relatin' to her, that everythin' would turn out OK. I don't think ya can just leave sick people alone. You gotta keep them in touch with what's happenin'. They may not look like they're listenin' but deep down inside I believe there's somethin' in there that's takin' it all in. It's like you're throwing a tow rope from ya brain into theirs.

Mickey was still here an' I could see his eyes was beginnin' to go deep into his head. I ain't looked in the mirror for a coupla days but I'm sure I was in the same boat. But what I looked like didn't matter an' I gotta little closer to the bedside lamp an' kept readin' to Adrian.

" '. . . And I rode the horses ahead. The rain was now fallin' heavy. We figured that the chances for a flash flood to come roaring down the gulch . . .' "

"Visiting hours are over, Mr. Balboa," a nurse said.

I had argued with this nurse maybe ten times to let me just stay there, to just forget I was there. I was even gonna threaten her a couple times, but I didn't want to upset the air around Adrian, if you know what I mean. So I just nodded, stuck my book into my back pocket, an' me an' Mickey walked out.

As I was going through the door, Mickey tapped me on the arm and says, "Ya hungry?"

The next day I was again sittin' beside Adrian's bed. I was still readin' from this book and from Adrian, who hadn't moved at all. It was like she was frozen, but I knew as long as she was breathin' she was listenin' to me, so that's all I had to know.

I turned the page of the book an' caught a glance of Mickey sittin' there. A little piece of sun was comin' through the shades and cuttin' across his face, and I could see poor Mick was lookin' old and feelin' very, very tired. I wished I could say somethin' to keep up his spirits, too, but all I could think about was my wife.

" '. . . so Jim rode on, aware that the desert was ahead . . .' " The sun had already left the sky a few hours ago, and I was tryin' to read by Adrian's nightlight that was hangin' over her bed. I was findin' it hard to keep readin', 'cause I knew any second the nurse would be comin' in an' tellin' me I gotta leave. When I heard those nurse's feet comin', I just stood up, an' me an' Mickey headed for the chapel.

As we went to the chapel, I felt I was becomin' very familiar with this here chapel. I liked the way it made me feel. It kinda wrapped itself around my body an' told me everythin' was okay, and then I would walk into the chapel an' look at all the angels an' the drawin's on the wall, an' Jesus nailed to the cross, an' all the things that make a chapel a chapel. I usually felt very down, but after a little while in there, my tank was full again. I felt more strong, y'know; I felt I could believe an' believe an' it

would come true. I just had what they call faith.
I was thinkin' about all this faith stuff when somethin' new came into my eyes. I seen Mickey move
over to the other side of the chapel and do somethin'
very different.

Mickey started to pray.

Adrian was still in what them doctors call a state
of comatose, an' still I didn't wanna believe that.
Adrian had been going through a lot of work an'
problems with Paulie, with me an' the kid an' tryin'
to keep me on the up-and-up, an' I just think she
was tired. And the body's a strange thing! I know
when I be fightin' an' I get hurt, sometimes the body
would just shut down, and there's nothin' ya can
do about it. I heard about people sometimes goin'
temporary blind, temporary deaf, temporary insane.
It was just temporary because the body's just healin'
itself, so I felt that—no, I mean I *knew* that Adrian
was temporary comatose.

I touched the back of her hand an' it made me
feel good. Her skin was so much like touchin' a
warm nylon scarf or somethin' like that. I been
thinkin' about somethin' nice to do for Adrian, and
that night in the chapel I found some paper towels
an' a pencil an' I wrote down this poem. Ya might
say this was very unusual for a human like me to
do such. Y'know, there was a coupla guys in school
who wasn't even full-fledged poets, they was kind of
part-time poets, an' everybody would shoot paper
clips at their heads an' give 'em lumps an' punch
'em on the arm an' call 'em fruitcakes an' everythin'.
It's tough to be a poet in a tough neighborhood.
Now here I was, tryin' to write 'cause Adrian liked
that stuff.

Even though I was kind of a lamebrain, I tried to

put some words together that made it rhyme,
y'know, kind of like a first-class TV commercial. I
opened up this brown paper towel that I had all
bunched in my hand, and I was gonna have to read
it pretty soon to Adrian because I was smearin' the
words all over the place. I held the paper towel
closer to the light an' said, "Here's somethin' I just
wrote for ya . . .

> Remember when we was on ice skates,
> I thought you were supposed to be great,
> But I kept giving you lip,
> And you kept trying to slip
> So I could catch you . . .
> That was our first date.
> After that every day was great.
> So now I want you to know
> That wherever you go,
> Atlantic City or in the snow,
> Don't worry about a thing,
> 'Cause as long as you wear this ring,
> I'll always be there to catch it . . ."

It was night again, an' night was always the worst
time for me. Night always felt heavy, an' I could
hear things that I couldn't hear durin' the day. Like
I could hear the buildin' moanin' an' groanin', an'
people's high heels cloggin' along the floor, an' all
of a sudden the clock started to sound like it was a
cheap coffee grinder just worryin' away up there on
the wall, an' pipes in the walls made noises that
could drive anybody nuts. I was so tired of tryin' to
get through to Adrian, y'know, communicate with
her, that I was restin' my face next to her hand,
tryin' to stay awake, but I was passin' out. I knew
I couldn't stay awake much longer, and the nurse

was gonna come in and throw me out and yell at me again for puttin' my face on her bed, but I didn't care any more. I just held Adrian's hand across my face an' kissed it an' began to drift. I felt myself goin' upside down, driftin' right out the window, and my body was kinda lookin' down at benches outside the Pennsylvania Hospital, an' I started to look down on Locust Street an' I was even gettin' higher than them trees now, an' I liked the way it felt an' I was hopin' I wouldn't have to land. Yeah, I was goin' higher an' faster, an' before I knew it I'd seen the whole Philly city. I didn't know where I was goin', but I didn't wanna stop. I figured this was where Adrian had gone an' I was comin'.

Somethin' hit me.

I stopped flyin'.

Somethin' hit me again. I started to sink back to the city an' past City Hall, back into the hospital window. I opened my eyes an' I seen Adrian's fingers movin' against my face. Her fingers touched my cheek again an' I got scared. I hoped this was real, 'cause I couldn't stand it if it weren't. She had to come back. I looked past her hand an' up her arm an' at her eyes.

They opened.

They opened!

I wanted to cry!

I wanted to jump, I wanted to scream, I wanted to break somethin'. I wanted to fly out that window like I had just done a second before, but I just put my head next to Adrian's face an' said, "I knew you'd come back."

32

WELL, IT LOOKED like everybody was gathered at
Adrian's hospital room. They was celebratin' an'
havin' a kinda sterilized party. I say sterilized because I had to make sure nobody had a cold or
nothin' before they come to this little get-together;
otherwise I would've had to bar 'em at the door,
if y'know what I mean. I think me an' Adrian had
enough sickness in our relationship. But even though
Adrian was sick, I had to admit she looked as
though God had painted her the healthiest face I'd
ever seen. Her hair was shiny brown an' her eyes
were brown as could be an' there was color in her
cheeks, and her skin was smooth and she was
smilin' and her lips weren't dry no more; an' she
had this ribbon in her hair. She looked like a big
toy to me.

"You haven't seen the baby, Rocky?" Adrian
said.

"No, I waited to see him together," I answered
and wondered if I'd said the right thing.

Gazzo come over an' smacked me on the back

an' said, "I seen it, doll, it's a winner, he's got your forearms," Gazzo finished sayin' an' started to tug the top of a cork off a champagne bottle. When he said the baby had my forearms, I was kinda worried, because I didn't know if I wanted anythin' that big on a baby. He would've looked like Popeye from the start, and everyone knows how tough it is to get through school if you got anything that stands out a little different. Even if it's a cowlick, the other kids are gonna bomb ya for it, so imagine havin' big forearms at the age of five. I knew I had to be kinda tired to be thinkin' these stupid thoughts.

I seen the nurse come in holdin' somethin' in the blanket. I couldn't believe it might be the baby. Y'know how sometimes ya *see* what's comin' an' ya *know* what's comin', but you can't believe what's comin' 'cause it's just too important to really be happenin'. She handed the little package to Adrian an' I was stiff. I felt like a cinder block fell on my head. I inched closer to Adrian an' looked down to the baby. My breath got very hot.

"That's really ours, he's ours?" I said.

"He's beautiful . . . Thank you, Rocky," Adrian said.

"C'mon, you did all of the work . . . I can't believe we done this."

"Believe me, we did."

"Oh, no, he don't have a name— Whaddaya wanna name him?"

Paulie come up an' put his arm around me and said, "Paulie's a good name."

"Yeah, it's nice," I said an' was hopin' he'd forget he made that suggestion.

"How about after the father?" Adrian said. And I couldn't believe she had done that either. Rocky,

Jr.? Rocky's a name you always kept for dogs or horses or things that like to get hit a lot and were tough, y'know?

"Rocky, Jr.? C'mon, you wanna do that?" I said.

Adrian nodded, an' after all she'd been through, I wasn't about to deny her nothin'.

"He's the best I ever seen . . . thanks, Adrian, ya done real good."

"Rocky, you look so tired, why don't you go get some sleep?" Adrian said.

I might've looked tired, but I didn't feel that tired. I just felt kind of hazy, y'know, dizzy, but not too tired. I leaned down and kissed the baby, then leaned up an' kissed Adrian an' said, "I'm okay. Y'know, Adrian, he's the best I ever seen . . . Listen, I been thinkin'. If you don't want me mixin' with Creed, we'll make out doin' somethin' else."

"There's only one thing I'd like you to do for me. Come here," Adrian said.

I leaned closer to Adrian and said, "What?"

"You know what I want you to do for me?"

"What?" I said again.

"Win!" she said.

Even from behind me I could feel Mickey's face go great, and he come forward, grabbed me around the waist, held his fist up in front of my face, and said, "Then what the hell are we waitin' for?!"

33

I RAN DOWN the steps of my house, hit that front door like it were made outta nothin', an' got out on that street an' started to run like I hadn't run since the first fight. The whole thing felt new to me, almost like I'd never done it before, one foot in front of the other foot, in front of the other foot, back an' forth, lungs startin' to burn, arms pumpin' back an' forth, back an' forth. I felt my arms startin' to swell. The feelin' almost felt new to me, but it's not, I've done this a million times. But like I says, the whole thing felt kinda like brand-new, like I just been unwrapped, and this thing called fightin' was all new to me again.

I just couldn't wait to get to the gym an' start workin' on that speed bag, 'cause that speed bag would come poundin' off my fists: one, two, one, two, one, two, one, two, one, two, three, four, one, two, three, four, one, two, three, four. An' the faster I would go, the more powerful it would sound, until finally it was a part of my body. Sometimes I thought the speed bag was gonna break my eardrums with its poundin', an' its poundin' was never changed. It never got softer, it always got louder an' faster an' meaner, an' the meaner you got, the meaner the bag got. About the speed bag, these psychologists say it's just you comin' back at yourself. It gives you back one hundred percent of what you gave it, an' I gave it one hundred percent of myself, an', God, it was givin' it back to me an' I loved it!

After the speed bag, I knew where I'd end up next, and I was hangin' upside down from a wall rack doin' Roman situps with Mickey poundin' my stomach with the side of his hands. He cupped his fists an' smacked 'em against my gut so that I thought the skin was tearin'. It hurt. The pain was worth it all.

The next thing we done was go back to chasing that chicken in the yard. The same chicken that had humiliated me a few weeks ago. Now it was me an' him. Chickens was maybe the toughest thing I'd ever seen in the world to catch because they ain't got much of a brain an' who knows what they're thinkin'. But I was gonna catch that chicken if I had to dive in this ground a hundred times. I was gonna catch this chicken until I had my whole head covered with scabs if it was necessary. I seen the chicken comin' toward me. He was gonna try to move along the right fence. I used a boxin' motion an' slid to the right. He started to go to the left, I slid to the left. It was back and forth, back and forth. Every move the chicken was doin' I was doin', which is good 'cause that's just what I wanted to do to Creed. I started backin' that bird into the corner, left, right, right, left, left side, left side, right side, until finally he was at the very back of that

cage an' I snatched down with my right hook an'
grabbed him around the neck an' flung him in the
air, an' as it was fallin' down I heard Mickey laugh.
God, it was great to hear him laugh at somethin'
I was doin' an' not at me in general.

Back in the gym again, it was late in the afternoon, and I was gettin' a little tired and I was
comin' to one of the hardest parts of my workout.
I was standin' dead center as Johnny was poundin'
that medicine ball into my stomach. The kid was
really feelin' his oats that day, because I thought
he was gonna knock my stomach right out through
my back an' have it stuck on the wall somewhere.
But I took it and I took it, and I kept on takin' it
with pleasure, 'cause I knew if I could take this, I
could probably take the beatin' that Creed was
gonna try to definitely put all over my body.

C'mon, Johnny, keep throwin'!

Keep throwin'!

Right before the workout ended, Mickey had
Johnny do somethin' I never seen anybody do before. Johnny was suppose ta blow these bubbles in
the air, and as they were fallin' down, I was suppose
ta break them with jabs an' hooks an' crosses an'
everything in my arsenal. I felt kind of stupid, but
I also felt like I was doin' somethin' wrong, because
the bubbles looked so beautiful floatin' there, in the
little bit of sunlight that was comin' into the gym.
But I done what I was told an' I was breakin' these
here bubbles like nobody ever broke bubbles before.
I don't know what good it was gonna do, because
when I hit Creed, one thing for sure was he weren't
just gonna go pop an' turn into no wet spot on the
floor.

The skip rope was never one of my strong suits.

I was the kind of guy who was always keepin' his feet very low to the floor, so, y'know, I always had that rope wrapped around my ankles, lookin' very stupid. But I worked with that rope hour after hour after hour, an' Mickey showed me how to get on my toes an' bounce around an' think light.

Think speed.

Think lightning.

An' the more I worked the better I got, until finally me and that rope was real buddies, 'cause it was just skippin' around faster than I'd ever moved before in my life. I was jumpin' higher an' double-jumpin' an' flippin' to the side. Y'know, if somebody had shown me all this stuff earlier in my life, or if I had tried to do all this stuff earlier in my life, how much better off I would've been at this point in my life. But I didn't wanna get into no deep problems or deep thinkin' now, 'cause the only thing I wanted to think about was Creed.

After a rubdown an' a little rest, Mickey had me pressin' a hundred-pound barbell in front of my neck an' behind my neck, in front of my neck, behind my neck, as Mickey was yellin', "Push, push, push!" Then he run me over to the heavy bag an' I punched

and punched

and punched.

Until my knuckles was gonna explode underneath them gloves. But I wasn't about to complain; I waited too long for this an' done everythin' Mickey wanted me to do. If Mickey said, "I want you to go over there an' eat five bricks for lunch," I'd ask him where the salt was.

I was doin' everythin' I was told to do, so I didn't have no excuses this time. I didn't want all the people who was now standin' around me as I was doin' these one-arm pushups in the middle of the ring. Y'know, it's funny, of all the exercises I would do around the gym, this is the one that everybody use ta watch, like it was somethin' special. I told 'em that it ain't no big deal; if you get out and just try, you'd probably be able to do it, 'cause I never done it before the last fight. I was just gonna do some regular pushups, y'know, then I thought I'd do somethin' maybe kinda funny for Mickey, an' I started doin' these here one-arm pushups, an' before I knew it, it had become a specialty.

At the end of the day Mickey really had some hard things set up for me to do. Now he wanted me to go in the ring an' catch that speedy lightweight who made me look so stupid last time. This is one of the shiftiest guys I'd ever seen. I'd move to the left, an' before I knew it, he was around behind me pattin' me on the butt. But last time I had a lot on my mind, y'know, I had my problems with Adrian, but now I put my eyes in the center of his chest an' followed him. He wasn't about to fake me out. If he moved, I moved.

I was his shadow.

And I kept thinkin', You can be faster than this guy, just tell your body to move faster. Tell your legs to move before his move. I kept thinkin', You're a spider, ya got this guy in the corner an' you're a big spider an' he's not gettin' out nowhere. He's the fly an' you're the spider. He moved, I moved. He jumped, I jumped. I zeroed in on him. He moved to the left and I nailed him. He moved to the right an' I nailed him against the turnbuckle, an' if he had been Creed, he would've been all mine. I grabbed this little guy around the waist an' lifted him over my head, then I sat him down an' patted him on the butt an' turned to Mickey, an' he yelled, "That's speed!"

I was headin' into the last part of my trainin', buildin' up my legs. I don't know if many people know about what happens to fighters, but the first thing that starts to defunk on them is their pins, y'know, the legs. I don't know why, but it's really strange the way nature is. Y'ever notice how, when a baby's born, his legs are all kind of like bent up pretty bad-lookin', an' they're usually, in my estimation, the last part of the body that kinda gets straightened out an' strong? So you figure they would last the longest 'cause they was the last things to be put in good working condition by nature. But wrong! The legs was the first thing to go sour on an athlete. When you start hittin' ya' thirties, it's like somebody poured sand an' Jello into your leg muscles, 'cause that's what can happen. But now I was outside on the streets breathin' that cold air in my lungs and tryin' to pump all that Jello an' sand out of my legs. I started to run to the marketplace, it was always one of my favorite spots 'cause the people always talked to each other an' dogs would run in the streets, an' it was kind of a carnival, 'cept it didn't have no rides, just had a lot of fish stands and fruit carts and unusual eatables. First time I run through this market, only a year ago, just a couple people waved at me. This time it was a parade of faces that waved me through, and they tossed a couple of pieces of fruit at me. I seen a couple kids start followin' me through the street like I was some Pied Piper, y'know.

I started passin' over a small bridge that was about three miles from the market. My legs were startin' to ache, but I knew in a little while I'd click over into that place where legs don't hurt no more.

I was pumpin' hard an' I could feel my T-shirt, underneath me, stickin' to my chest an' makin' a warm, wet feel as I stretched one foot in front of the other, one foot in front of the other. I turned around and I seen there was at least twenty kids followin' me now. That made me run even faster. Y'know how embarrassed I would've been if some kid, who only come up to, say, my knees, started passin' me. If somebody got a picture of that an' gave it to Mickey, Mickey would come over an' use my head for a bongo drum. An' y'know how kids are, they're always tryin' to show off, but the closer they come to me, the faster I'd go. But I kinda liked this feelin' like a rabbit an' them bein' the grey-hounds. I decided to head for the museum steps and swung my way toward the parkway.

I couldn't believe what was happenin' there. By the time I got to the Ben Franklin Parkway, it looked as though I had every Boy Scout an' kid in the whole city followin' me. There must've been a couple hundred kids keepin' pace with me. When we crossed the streets, the traffic would stop an' stop an' stop, 'cause there must've been kids two hundred feet back just stacked on the parkway.

I don't know if I deserved all this attention, y'know. I don't know what happened durin' that last fight, that so many people looked to me for some kind of example. That I did somethin' they would wanna do or they are gonna do, an' I felt I had a lot of responsibilities this time. Not just to me and Adrian, but to all these kids, an' maybe people that are a little older, who would like to run along but just didn't have it in the legs no more, but had it in the spirit. It made me feel good, but it also made me feel kinda scared at the same time.

I could see the museum steps gettin' closer an' I could feel the ground vibrate a little bit with all those hundreds of little feet hoofin' behind me.

Who was I?

What was I supposed to do now?

I mean, really, I'm just a ham-and-egger who got lucky. I might be a little faster an' a little stronger now, but I'll never think of myself as a champion or a fighter's fighter. I wanna win this fight now, but the belt don't mean everythin' to me. My life is back in my house, that's what means everythin'. This is just somethin' I wanna do for me. It's almost like an experiment, 'cause I always believed in my little brain that if ya got, y'know, the basic tools an' you're willin' to sacrifice all the good times for hard times, you're gonna usually end up rewardin' ya'self with great times. I wanna see if anywhere the brain can take you, ya can really do what ya think you can do. What I mean by all that mumbo jumbo is, the most important part of an athlete's body, an' I guess any part of anybody's body, is the brain. Without the brain you're nothin' but a lot of meat stacked on bones. There ain't no motor, there ain't no fire in the furnace. I spent a lot of time walkin', always tryin' to do things that would make my mind a little stronger. I mean, I would stare at a star without blinkin' for an hour. Even my eyes would start to tear and burn, but I would keep doin' it 'cause I figured that might come in handy someday if I ever got into a starin' contest with somebody on a bus or subway. Or squeezin' a rubber ball until I felt the veins in my forearm was gonna come right through my leather coat an' splash all over me. Yeah, I always trained myself to do things that was uncomfortable because I knew they would all come in handy.

The first time me an' Creed fought, he hit me punches that I never thought in my life I could take. But the more he hit, the more I knew I could take his beatin's, 'cause I had taken so much pain before that I was used to it. And I welcomed it. I wanted him to give me everythin' he had. I wanted to go into that shower at the end of the fight knowin' that I had taken his best an' that he had taken my best. And oh, boy, God, ya wouldn't believe, y'know, how hard this guy could whack! Somewhere in the second or third round he whacked me with a left hook an' I coulda swore my eyeball had fell out. I was for a second gonna hold my glove up to see it. My eye had come out, but in a second I knew that was kinda stupid, because the eye is really kinda bolted in there by nature.

We was just a few feet away from the steps an' I started across the street, followed by what looked like five hundred, a thousand, ten thousand, who knows? There was a lotta kids out there an' they was doin' everythin' I was doin'. I hit that first step an' started to really sprint. The steeper they got, the harder I pumped, an' the kids pumped along with me. These steps were the most beautiful steps I ever run up. They seemed like they would just keep goin' right into heaven. That's right, I think the guy who built this place was headin' toward heaven, except he ran outta concrete. But I was pumpin' an' I could feel my lungs burnin' an' my legs was sayin' *stop, stop, stop* but my brain was sayin' *go, go, go,* an' I tightened my jaw an' pushed to the next level, then to the next level, takin' four steps at a time, an' finally I seen the last landin' an' I sprinted as hard as I could, took that in two strides, got up to the top, an' felt just like I done the first time!

Better!

I raised my hands an' started to dance around, lookin' down on the city, knowin' I was in the best shape of my life an' this was the best city in the world an' these kids were the best an' nothin' could be better at this moment. There's somethin' that happens when your body's in the best shape it could ever be in an' your mind is right. Ya just feel like nothin' could beat ya. The only thing that could beat ya would be ya'self.

I felt so good I could scream an' yell an' cry an' do everythin' loud at one time. I jumped as high as I could an' I looked around an' all the kids were raisin' their hands an' jumpin' around, an' it was like we was all dancin' to the same song. There was no music, there was no band, there was no whaddaya call it, guest soloist, but we was all dancin'.

34

I WAS BACK at our house. It was about eight o'clock at night an' everythin' was very quiet. I was in the baby's room. I was rockin' the baby in this little rockin' chair that we bought, an' the floor was creakin' a little bit, but the kid just finished his bottle an' was out to the world, an' no creakin' rockin' chair was gonna ever change that. So I figured, if that noise didn't wake him up, maybe I could hum a little bit. There's somethin' really nice about hummin' to ya' kid. I know it's corny, an' somethin' that only Mother Goose should do, but I liked hummin' to my kid, an' hum I did 'til I knew he was really doin' some deep sleepin', an' I stood up as quiet as I could, moved across them creakin' boards, an' lowered my baby into his crib. I made sure his head was turned to the side, just like Adrian showed me, an' he was lyin' on his stomach lookin' very peaceful. I looked down at his hands an' kept wonderin' how I coulda ever been that tiny, y'know. I touched his hands with my finger an' listened to him breathe a couple times an' said, "You're gonna have it all . . ."

After I put the baby to bed, I moved down the hallway an' almost slipped on a throw rug that Adrian had put down there, an' I walked into our bedroom. When I opened the door, I seen Adrian was lyin' on the bed readin'. She seen me and smiled.

"How's the baby?"

"He's got no complaints . . ." I said and sat on the bottom of the bed. I leaned against one arm an' looked at her just for a second. We looked at each other for a few more seconds, an' I was really startin' to feel comfortable just starin' back and forth when she said, "Rocky, close your eyes."

"What is it?"

"Just close your eyes, Rocky."

I closed both my lamps an' I could feel Adrian shiftin' around on the bed an' leanin' over the side. Then I heard somethin' crinklin', like new paper, y'know. Y'know how new paper always crinkles. It's that famous crinkle sound.

"Okay," Adrian said, "you can open your eyes."

"What's this? It ain't Christmas," I said an' pulled the package close to me.

"Just open it."

Well, again I done what I was told, an' I opened the box, then I opened a second box, an' underneath that was some, y'know, toilet—whaddaya call it— *tissue* paper that was folded over real neat-like, an' I flipped that back an' I flipped the other piece back an' inside I seen somethin' black and shiny. I pulled out this beautiful pair of black boxing shorts, real satin. And on the side they had this yellow-gold trimmin', an' then underneath that, believe it or not, were these black and yellow shoes that matched, and a robe.

"They're beautiful . . ." I said.

"You really like them?"

"Oh, yeah . . . my favorite colors," I said and rubbed the satin trunks between my hands an' looked at my name stitched on the side. I was thinkin' that I had the best wife God ever put in the neighborhood.

She had it all.

But what she had the most was heart. I had to admit she was the best. "Y'know, Adrian, you're the best . . ." I said and kissed her.

I dunno, maybe around two or three in the mornin', I couldn't sleep no more. Matter of fact, I couldn't sleep at all, so I had a decision to make: either lay in bed with my eyes open, twitchin' around, or get up an' walk around an' maybe unwind. I was careful to make no noise an' moved downstairs an' didn't turn on no lights either. Since we still didn't have that much furniture, I wasn't worried about stubbin' an' breakin' my toe before the fight. That woulda been very embarrassin', too, to have them sportswriters say Rocky Balboa had to call the fight on account of a broken toe he got in the middle of the night when sneakin' through his house. I moved into the kitchen an' I leaned against the sink. It was very quiet. The only thing in there besides me an' the blackness was the hummin' of the refrigerator. I thought about what was gonna happen tomorrow night. This was, like Mickey said, my last shot. I kept thinkin' about the first fight over an' over, an' all the mistakes I made, an' the mistakes I knew Creed would never make again, not this time. He would be the perfect fightin' machine. I knew it. Creed would be out to destroy me.

Beat me bad.

Hurt me.

Pulverize the idea in anybody's head that I might've been a serious contender. I can't say I blame him. I don't blame 'im at all. The guy's gotta have a lotta pride; he's champ, right? But I was thinkin' about my responsibility to the kid sleepin' upstairs, my wife, an' Mickey, poor Mick. I knew they were gonna have to tie him down durin' the fight, 'cause he'd be in there swingin' with me every second.

Yeah, I just leaned against that sink an' listened to that refrigerator motor an' thought about how great that Creed was gonna be tomorrow night.

35

THE NIGHT OF the fight at the Philadelphia Spectrum was filled with more pageantry than ever seemed possible for a conservative city. The noise and the patriotism defied comparison. And the decor, which consisted of several fifty-foot posters of Apollo Creed and Rocky Balboa, lent more than a mere feeling of a Roman gladiatorial contest.

I stood over my kid's crib with Adrian. We weren't sayin' nothin', we were just starin' down at the baby. It was time to fight. I knew I heard duty callin' somewhere in the back of my head, so I just had to reach down an' touch one of the baby's little thumbs. ". . . guess I gotta go now," I said, me an' Adrian stepped out of the room.

I had all my gear packed up an' I headed down the stairway. My feet was feelin' very heavy, I don't know why. I guess I was a little scared. I wasn't scared of, y'know, fightin' Creed, or scared of anythin' like that. I was scared for the other people. I was scared for the wife an' baby, an' the people that

148

needed me, 'cause if I did get banged around an' my brain twisted for good, how were these people gonna take care of everythin'? . . . I mean, now I had become a responsible party in general.

Adrian didn't say nothin', but I could hear her thinkin'. Adrian was just standin' in the doorway lookin' at me, an' I could feel the cold startin' to tighten my face up. The cold kinda felt good, an' it looked like a perfect night for a fight. I liked the gray, an' I liked the invisible wind, an' the trees out in front of my house kinda looked the way I looked, or the way I felt, trimmed down to the bone.

I seen Paulie's face come up from behind Adrian, an' he blew some smoke outside and the wind just whipped it away.

"So, Paulie, you're gonna help out with the baby tonight, right?" I said.

"I'll handle everythin'."

"You just take care of everything, okay? . . . You still losin' weight?"

"Yeah, I'm on a good diet—you're gonna be late for your own fight."

"You'd better go," Adrian said an' touched my cheek.

"Then everythin's okay here," I said an' looked at Paulie an' held my finger up an' pointed in his face. "Paulie, you're in charge."

"I can handle the dumb house—go fight!"

"Everythin's fine, Rocky," Adrian said.

"Then I better get outta here," I said an' reached for my wife, an' we hugged. I could feel her body fittin' against mine. Me an' her fit together perfect.

". . . I love you," Adrian said.

". . . I love you—I'm gonna try, hard."

36

THE CROWD HAD almost completely filed into the Philadelphia Spectrum, and the arena seemed on the verge of bursting with an overabundance of humanity. Every available inch of space had a human being placed within it. Every so often a fight would erupt if anyone dared to venture so much as two feet away from his seat.

The commentators sat at ringside, flanked by cameras and the cream of the American sporting press. In front of them was a spectacularly decorated ring. The ropes had never before seen bright yellow set against a stark white canvas, with a sunburst effect in the center of the ring that consisted of a multitude of colors splashing out in every direction.

". . . for all those watching tonight's telecast, we think you're in for a real battle in every sense of the word," commentator Bill Baldwin said. "This rematch was never to take place. The champion has let it be known that he is in the best shape of his illustrious career, and as for Rocky Balboa, still a two-to-one underdog, a pile-driving street brawler from Philadelphia, can he duplicate his astonishing feat of ten months ago? Can he be the same after receiving an incredible beating at the hands of the champion? The experts say no . . . This reporter is not so sure."

Apollo's dressing room was stuffed with people, but these bodies made no impression on the champion that they were alive. Apollo's serious demeanor dictated that he wanted no distraction whatsoever from his deep thoughts. Only his wife, sitting nearby, dared have the confidence to meet his eyes. Except for various sighs of self-conscious breathing, the only other sound was the ripping hiss of Apollo Creed's hands being taped.

I was headin' toward the Philadelphia Spectrum, but I knew somethin' was goin' on in my brain. What I mean is, I knew I had to do somethin' before I went to the arena, an' no matter what, I was gonna do it. So I shot down pass York Avenue and headed toward the same church me an' Adrian was married in. I pulled the car over as quick as I could. I jumped out an' run up to the rectory. "Father Carmine! Yo, Father Carmine! You home?" I waited for a second and the window opened and a priest, who I'd always called Father Carmine, stuck his head out.

"Who is it?"

"Rocky Balboa!"

"What're you doing out there? Aren't you fighting tonight?"

"Absolutely—but I wanna ask ya a favor."

"Yes?"

"About the fight. Y'know, the family ain't got

nobody but me—so could ya throw down a blessin'
so if I get nailed bad tonight, y'know, it won't be
too bad—it won't be so permanent that I'll be
damaged in kind of a way that I'll be no good to
nobody no more."

I waited for a couple seconds, and I know the
Father was tryin' to figure out what I was sayin',
and once he done that he made the sign of the
cross and blessed me, and I felt a smile rip across
my face and started backin' away to the car.

"Thanks!" I turned, ran back to the front seat,
slammed the door, and drove away as fast as that
car was able to drive me away.

Commentator Bill Baldwin was glancing around
in his seat, looking at the people packed to the
rafters, and had a look of true amazement etched
across his face. "The arena is certainly packed with
Rocky's people—I never saw so many Italians in
one place in my life!"

"You said that, I didn't!" commentator Steward
Neham said and smiled.

"Many rumors have been circulated about this
fight." .

"That's right, Bill, the most obvious being a defi-
nite desire for Apollo to draw first blood and end
it quickly—proving his claim that their last fight
was a fluke. Again, I'm not so sure."

"There's bad blood here."

"That's an understatement, Bill."

I entered the dressing-room hallway, where all
the fighters stay, an' I seen the place like I never
seen it before. It looked like every inch of the joint
was lined with cops an' guys in white jackets that
had "Security" written on the back. I started to walk

fast, then I figured I might as well step on it since I was already goin' to get killed by Mickey an' started to run.

All these here guys were bein' very nice, sayin', "Go get 'im, Rock," "You can do it, Rock," "Knock 'im out, Rock!" I didn't know about knockin' him out, I was just hopin' I could get to the dressin' room without trippin' an' chippin' my teeth or somethin'.

Then I seen somethin' I knew I didn't want to see.

I seen Mickey up ahead of me kickin' a wall and cursin' to himself, lookin' around wonderin' where the heck I was. When he seen me comin' toward him, he threw up his hands and yelled, "I'm goin' to break your neck! Where have ya been?! Are you losing your brains? We got a fight here! Get the hell dressed!"

I was about to try to say somethin' in my defense, but I knew if I did, he might reach down my throat an' remove my tongue with his fingers, so I just walked through the doors an' headed to my dressing room; but before I got three steps, Creed come out of his doorway wearin' his robe. His hands were all taped up, an' he looked right into my face like he had somethin' important to say. Mickey didn't want any part of this stuff an' pulled my arm an' said, "Get in your dressing room, Rock!"

"I'd like to have a couple words with the Stallion," the champ said.

"This ain't right!" Mickey yelled and looked at me, but I nodded it was okay. I was really curious as to what Creed wanted to say to me, an' I figured two or three minutes either way wouldn't make much of a difference, y'know. So Mickey started to back away, but like Mickey always did, he yelled back to me, "I ain't takin' much more of this!"

"It's okay," I said and watched Mickey go into the dressing room.

". . . I just wanted to tell you I'm going out there to win big tonight and I hope you don't get hurt," Apollo said an' looked at me harder than he ever looked at me before.

"I hope so, too."

"The bad-mouthing in the press was nothing personal, it was just to get the public excited."

". . . pretty smart," I said and felt that dumb smile comin' out of my face, but there was nothin' I could do about it, so I just smiled dumb-like.

"I got respect for you, man, but I'm telling you, I'm going for the quick knockout."

After Apollo said that, he started to turn away, and I felt I had to say somethin', too, because I couldn't just let this guy insult me like that. "Hey, yo, Apollo," I said, and Apollo stopped and looked at me. "I'm gonna try an' win, too." Apollo laughed at me and walked back into his dressing room, and, like magic, Mickey stuck his head out and poked me in the chest with his finger.

"What the hell did he talk about?" Mickey yelled.

"Life in general."

At ringside, nearly every reporter was on the phone, and security guards were having the most difficult time trying to keep people from blocking the aisles that the fighters would soon use when entering the arena.

Commentator Steward Neham faced the television camera. "Tonight we are being broadcast to millions of viewers around the world! It might be interesting to note the fighters' records. The champion has forty-seven victories and no losses. The challenger has forty-four wins, twenty-one losses, and the only time he was off his feet was in the first fight with Apollo Creed."

I was in the bathroom leanin' against one of the sinks, prayin'. The only thing I could hear was the drippin' faucet and my heartbeat. I never heard my heart so loud. I wondered if Al and Mickey and Johnny, who was leanin' against the wall, could hear it, too. While I had the chance, I just prayed to God that everythin' would turn out okay, and if I was meant to win, I was very grateful, and if I was supposed to lose, as long as I did my best, I had nothing to complain about.

"It's time, kid," I heard Mickey's voice say.

I stood up, made the sign of the cross, and we all stepped out of the bathroom and headed toward the hallway leadin' to the ring. As we pushed through them doors at the end of the dressing-room hallway, I could hear the sound of the people gettin' louder and louder, and it kind of reminded me of the sound that you hear when you put one of them seashells up to your ears. It kept gettin' louder, and I could feel my guts startin' to tighten and I was glad I didn't eat nothin' before I come over here. I was really gettin' nervous, which was kind of backward for me, because I never got nervous about nothin' at the time. I always got nervous after what I was supposed to be nervous about was over. In other words, I was always a step behind, y'know. But tonight was different. Tonight I could feel my ankles turnin' into puddin', an' my calves were tight an' my knees felt like there was a couple of bugs buzzin' inside them, makin' them shake a little bit, an' my thighs felt like they were shakin' off the bone every time I took a step. I knew all this was in my mind, 'cause I was in the best shape of my life, but I was nervous an' couldn't stop my mouth from talkin' either.

"It's really warm for October, don't you think, Mickey?"

"No, it's perfect!"

"I wonder what the temperature is?" I asked.

"Whatever it is, it's perfect!"

"Y'know, my shoulder feels a little stiff.".

"You're in perfect working condition, now shut up!" Mickey shouted.

But I couldn't shut up, an' I knew I was makin' all the dumb excuses fighters make right before a fight, so in case they do lose, they can blame it on the weather or a stiff shoulder or a headache or a sore thumb or just life in general.

"Yo, Mick, while I got a chance, I wanna say I'm gonna try hard for you tonight . . ." I said and patted Mickey on the arm, and he seemed to like them words. Then I felt kinda shy for saying them and said, "Ain't this robe nice? Better than last year, that's for sure. It's kinda cute. I'm impressed with the robe. Adrian got it for me."

"Yeah, it's real adorable."

Commentator Steward Neham shifted around in front of the monitors, fired up a cigar, and saw the crowd beginning to convulse with excitement. He lowered the cigar and cleared his throat. "Yes, the crowd is beginning to stir as Rocky Balboa, known to millions as the Italian Stallion, is making his way toward the ring—the crowd is chanting his name. Why this fighter of limited ability has gained such popularity is still a mystery to me," he said and turned to the other commentator.

"Well, Stew, he'd better be in great shape, because he's in for the challenge of his life!"

"Again an understatement . . . but rumor has it that perhaps the champion is in too good of a shape. In other words, he could have overtrained, which is nearly as bad as undertraining, and only in the later rounds will that prove dangerous."

Paulie settled himself in front of the television and unscrewed the top of a beer bottle and swirled down the content in one long inhale. Without missing a beat, he reached for a pretzel that was in a dish positioned on his lap. Adrian, though she was still not up to her full strength, was dressed as though she were at the fight. She sat almost self-consciously on the corner of the couch, and her eyes flipped back from Paulie to the television and her own doubts about the outcome of this evening's fight. She straightened the front of her red dress and turned shyly toward her brother.

"Do you think it will be all right?"

"Would I be eatin' if anythin' was wrong?" Paulie said and belched. "Here he comes now!"

I seen what looked like a million hands. Yeah, every available hand that was in Philadelphia was wavin' as we bumped our way to the ring. I never felt so proud. I don't know why these people liked me so much, but I really felt proud to be in this city an' makin' so many people feel good. An' it didn't cost me a dime, which kinda made me feel good, too. I was wavin' back when I felt Mickey touch the back of my neck.

"These people are for you, Rock!!" he screamed into my ear.

"I appreciate it!"

"Tonight's our night—tonight you're gonna show the world who ya are! Tonight you're goin' to be unstoppable! Ya' the best. Ya' the best."

One of the commentators shifted his headphone into a more comfortable position and glanced down at the monitor. Though they had covered many of these fights, both commentators could not disguise the almost childlike enthusiasm in their voices.

"Apollo Creed should be making his entrance any second, and the crowd is becoming restless."

Again glancing down at the monitor, they saw what appeared to be a plastic wedge shield that split the people to one side of the aisle as Creed and his army of bodyguards moved toward the ring. This was in contrast to the time he had entered the ring dressed as George Washington, perched very comically on the bow of a cardboard ship. ". . . Apollo Creed seems to be in a very serious frame of mind."

"I've seen Creed fight many times, but I've never seen him so intense!"

I heard all the noise, and it was even louder than the noise they made for me, except there was much more booing going on. I knew Creed was comin' to the ring, an' I was hopin' that everyone wouldn't boo him, but this was my hometown and, like Creed said, he wanted to teach me a lesson in front of my people—so these people was giving him some of his own medicine. I leaned over to Mickey.

"It's Apollo!"

"Who did you expect?"

"Yeah, that's true."

The booing got louder, and I thought the hissing sound was gonna break the lights in the place by the time Creed got into the ring an' cut through the ropes. He moved like he was some big alley cat an' come over to me, and I seen his manager standing behind him holdin' up the gold championship belt and screaming how Apollo was the greatest!

"You in two . . . you're down in two!" Apollo said and walked away.

"Don't let it bother ya," Mickey said and patted my shoulder.

"Wouldn't it bother you?"

I was kind of proud of my robe, the way it looked all black and yellow and kinda shiny; but I could see Apollo was pretty proud, the way he stood in his white fightin' outfit. This time he wasn't wearin' the red, white, and blue flag robe, like he done last time. This time he was wearin' white an' red—my colors from the last fight. I don't know if he was tryin' to tell me somethin' by doin' that, but all I know is he looked mad. And I knew he was really mad, I mean gigantically mad, when one of his corner men held up a mirror so he could comb his hair and he pushed it away. Creed never pushed mirrors away. I took a deep breath an' looked over at the ring announcer as he walked to the center of the ring an' pointed at the timekeeper, who rung the bell two or three times. The Spectrum quieted down a little bit. Everybody was nervous tonight—it wasn't just me. The ring announcer wiped the sweat that was running down his face and grabbed the microphone like he really knew what he was doin', and held up his hand high and spoke in a voice as good as any guy I ever heard on the radio before. Yeah, he really had a nice voice.

"Ladies and gentlemen, welcome to the Philadelphia Spectrum!"

Well, he said the right thing, because everyone started applauding themselves an' I started applauding, and it was like one big, happy family, y'know.

"Without further delay, may I introduce the combatants for tonight's fight . . . In the far corner, weighing two hundred and two pounds, a man who thrilled the world last year—from the great fighting city of Philadelphia, the Italian Stallion, Rocky Balboa!"

I stepped forward and took a bow and kinda smiled as much as I could and felt a little wet under my robe. Why am I lying? I felt so nervous I thought I was going to throw up.

"Now, in the far corner, a champion who needs no introduction anywhere in the civilized world, weighing in at two hundred and twenty pounds— the true master of disaster, the undefeated heavyweight of the world, the one, the only, Apollo Creed! ! !"

I heard a big roar go up, spotted with a lot of boos, an' Apollo didn't wave at the crowd. What he wanted to do was get at me. I could tell that because he kept curlin' up his lip every time he looked at my corner. The timekeeper rang the bell, and the referee waved us to the center of the ring, so me and Al Silvanni headed to the center, and as I got there, he slipped off my robe and put the mouthpiece in. Apollo had his mouthpiece in, and there we were starin' at each other from six inches away. He was so big I couldn't believe it. His muscles had muscles, and then they had grown even more muscles. He looked like a real museum piece.

"You both know the rules," the referee started to say, and Apollo leaned close to me.

"You're going down," Apollo said, louder than the referee was speaking.

"No holding behind the neck."

"I pity you!" Apollo yelled.

"In the case of a knockout, go to a neutral corner," the referee said, and then I ignored Apollo.

"In two—you in two!"

"And come out fighting," the referee concluded and waved us away.

"Get ready for the storm, chump!" Apollo said and smacked my gloves and turned back to his corner.

I felt this lump gettin' kinda big in my throat as I moved back to my corner, but I forgot all about it when I seen Mickey. I was really goin' to try for this old guy, that's for sure.

"He's still upset, Mick."

"Who cares! Remember, protect that eye! Speed, move, jab, and hook! But no matter what, don't go back to fightin' southpaw! I'll tell ya when! Now get him!"

"I'll try."

"Good luck, Rock," Johnny said and took the buckets outta the ring and got ready for the bell. Mickey was just about out of the ring and I was startin' to kneel to say a last-minute prayer, y'know, when he leaned close to me and said, "He's gonna try to kill you, but get through this round and he's ours!"

Mickey finally stepped off the edge of the ring, and I said a little somethin' to God, y'know, an' then I heard the bell go off. This was it. I made the sign of the cross, whipped myself up, turned around, and got "ready for the storm." Before I knew what happened, Creed was on me. He hit me with three straight left hands, a right, and a left hook so fast I thought I'd been hit by a piece of lightning. Then he backed off an' waved for me to chase him. I know he could have kept beatin' on me for a long time. He had me off balance, that's for sure. I never figured him to come on so strong, that's not his style. He kinda waits back, picks you apart, an' then knocks ya dead. Yeah, he was gonna show me his mean side in front of all these people. I went after him an' he tagged me with five quick jabs. I was bobbin' an' weavin', but every punch he threw found my face. I tried to cut him off after we had gone around the ring once, but he nailed me with double hooks an' switched directions again an' hit me with six or seven jabs that felt like they was goin' through my face. Creed was tellin' the truth. He wasn't in shape for the last fight.

God, he was tough!

And, God, he hit hard!

God help me.

I heard Mickey screamin' when I passed by my corner. "Lean right! Break his damn jab!" I tried to cut him off, but Creed was movin' like he had rockets on his feet. He was the fastest thing I ever seen, but I was gonna catch him. I didn't know when, y'know, but as long as I was awake, I was gonna catch him.

One commentator cleared his throat, adjusted his headset, glanced back and forth between the TV monitors, and spoke out in a very excited, professional manner. "I don't believe it! The southpaw from Philly is now fighting right-handed—he's also faster than last time, but so is the champion. Balboa is taking a thrashing."

"Bill, I hate to admit it, but it does look like a mismatch, and I'm curious about Rocky's right eye. Apollo's hooks appear to be landing at will," the second commentator remarked.

"They certainly do! Oh, the champion has never looked better and madder!"

Apollo slammed Rocky back into Rocky's corner and began to work him over. His combinations were thrown with hairsplitting accuracy, and every punch was geared to cut and jar the challenger into a sense of unconsciousness. The challenger, having no other alternative, grabbed the champion's arms to postpone the slaughter. Creed pushed him away and tapped him on the forehead with his gloves and yelled, "Go down! I'm gonna put you down!" The champion began to back off and box in the uniform manner. Jab after jab after jab continually found its mark. But the real damage was being done with the left hook, a punch that Apollo had rarely used in the first encounter with Rocky Balboa. But now the left hooks seemed to be landing at will and were certainly causing increasing damage to Rocky's already questionable eye. Creed finally caused Rocky to throw an amateurish left hook, and he cut loose with two left-right combinations, another left-right combination, three hooks, two rights, and Balboa appeared to be on his way to dream street—when suddenly he exploded with hooks to the body and head and drove the champion halfway across the ring. Maintaining his balance, Creed leaned to the right and again caused Balboa to throw an amateurish overhand left that propelled him into the ropes. As Balboa bounced back off the ropes, Creed was waiting with a stiff right hand that nearly jarred the challenger off his feet. Creed exploded with a series of three hooks and rights that left Rocky just teetering on the brink of consciousness. As the challenger groped forward, Creed threw a stiff, upswinging left uppercut that nearly tore the challenger's head off, and Rocky spun to the floor.

Feeling the canvas beneath him awakened Balboa's fighting instincts, and he was instantly on his feet. Disgusted that he had been knocked down so early in the battle, Balboa shook his head in almost an apologetic way. The crowd was screaming his name, hoping for a miracle, some unexpected, magical punch that would daze the champion and perhaps put Balboa back into the fight. As the referee finished the mandatory eight-count, Creed wasted no time in rushing across the ring to throw a devastating right that nearly floored Rocky again, and followed it up with three left-right combinations that had Rocky again on dream street, and finally three left hooks that dumped Rocky in his corner.

I couldn't believe I was down. I couldn't believe I had been dumped twice in the first round, and I had seen every punch coming.

This was gettin' embarrassin'! I could hear Mickey screamin' somethin'. I could hear thousands of people yellin' my name. But none of them knew what was going on inside my head. Creed was tryin' to kill me, no doubt about it. Every punch had dynamite on it. I didn't have to touch my nose to know it was broken, an' I felt somethin' warm comin' down the side of my face, and I knew he had cut my eye again. I seen Creed go back to the neutral corner, and he was smilin' and wavin' at the crowd, and that kinda made me mad. I got up, took a deep breath, and waited for Creed to come on. If he was gonna take me out, let him do it toe-to-toe, an' not stand back there wavin' an' wastin' his time tryin' to embarrass me.

The referee moved his hands, which said we start fightin' again, and Creed come after me. He threw a left that I ducked, a right that hit me. He hit me with another left-right, but he missed a hook an' I saw my openin' an' I cut loose with a shot to the body and two left hooks to the head that sent him against the ropes. He bounced back and caught me with a stiff right hand and waved for me to come to the center of the ring. I knew he was setting me up and I should have covered up, but I didn't care. If he was gonna take me out, let him take me out clean, but I wasn't running, I was gonna take his best—that's all there was to it.

"He must be in great shape to be withstanding this butchering. And that's what it is, a butchering!" one commentator yelled into his microphone.

Apollo went after the challenger with a vengeance. With the red light on the ring post indicating that there were only ten seconds left to go in the round, Creed cut loose with a series of hooks, a series of straight right hands, and two more left hooks that had Rocky gasping for breath. But the challenger survived the round and started back to his corner. Before he had gone three feet, his corner men were in the ring and guiding him back to the stool.

Paulie opened another beer without taking his eyes off the television and mumbled to himself, "I'll break his head, break his head," he said and looked at his sister. "Don't start cryin'. Things are gonna be okay. It's only the first round."

Adrian rubbed her eyes and looked away.

"I can't believe it," I said and looked at Mickey. "What?"

"He broke my nose again!" I said and let Al try to close the cut.

Apollo Creed stood in his corner, not even botherin' to take his seat. He had all the earmarks of a man who realized he controlled the fight and could take out his opponent at a moment's notice. The booing and cursing he was receiving from the thousands of hometown fans made him smile even more broadly. The trainer leaned close to the champion. "Did his switching styles throw you off?"

"No way."

"Then you should have had him! Hook off the jab! I told you not to let up—don't let him cut the ring off! The man is still dangerous! Hear?"

"Dangerous, nothing!"

"He's dangerous!"

"Two, he's through in two! He was lucky!"

"You better pay attention to that man over there!" his trainer insisted.

I sat in my corner tryin' to figure out what I should do for the next round. I didn't think the switchin' styles was throwin' the guy off very much; he had almost beat me to death, y'know. The game plan was kinda backfirin'. I looked up at Mickey. "I want to go back to my old style," I said.

"We got a plan, we stay to it, damn it! I'll tell you when! You'll get your rhythm soon!"

"Yeah?"

"Think you can't be hurt! You can't, you're tough —the toughest!"

"He's great, Mick!"

"He's just a man—he's no better than you—you can beat him! You're a tank! Think you're a tank! Go through him!"

The commentators exchanged notes and looked directly into the monitor. "Rocky Balboa is a more sophisticated fighter, but he's taking a terrific beating. The big question is, how much effect has it had? We'll soon see—here's the bell now."

I sat in my corner takin' deep breaths, still tryin' to figure out Creed's speed. It's funny how fast you can think when ya' hurt. It's like there's part of ya' brain that's tryin' to save ya' life. And that's what I needed right now. This guy was bent on makin' me hamburger.

I heard Mickey say, "How's his eye, Al?"

Al put his fingers on a warm spot over my eye and said, "Bad."

It wasn't that bad. Yeah, it hurt a little bit, but that's the name of the game—pain. Fightin' is really kind of simple. It's all mathematics. It's ya' job to hit more than ya got hit. Simple, huh? "Everything's okay," I said.

"He's gonna floor you!"

"I ain't goin' down no more, Mickey. Can I have my mouthpiece?"

After years in the ring, y'know exactly when the bell's gonna ring, an' I knew it was only a couple seconds away, so I tensed my legs an' got ready to rush across the ring. I was goin' to really take it to Creed, step inside his offense and land to his body. And I mean land! That was my only shot, 'cause if he kept me at a distance, he was definitely gonna bounce me off the planet Pluto. The guy really had my number, no doubt about that. The bell rung, an' I rushed across the ring, an' Creed danced out of his corner an' I think he jabbed me 'bout six times. I don't know why I was countin' at a time like this. But I estimate six times. He was laughin' at me an' puttin' his hand on my forehead an' firin' straight rights into my eye. What got me so mad was that I knew what he was gonna do, but I couldn't do nothin' about it.

Did you ever feel like that?

It's a bad feelin' in general.

He moved forward, lowerin' his head, kinda makin' fun of my style; then he stood up straight, an' that's when I come after him. I thought I had

trapped Creed against the ropes, but he spun an'
whacked me with three quick left jabs and a
smackin' bollo punch. That was somethin' new. I
hate surprises like that. And the last punch rocked
me straight up, y'know. Then I got mad an' pushed
Creed backwards and got him against the ropes.
He tried to get away, but I cut him off and pushed
him back and hit him with a real hard left-right
combination to the body, and he covered up. This
was exactly what I wanted him to do. Here I came!
I hit him with two left hooks on the arms an' felt
them really dig into the bone, then followed with
a right uppercut to the body an' double hooks to
the head. Creed covered up, so I tried to pull his
hand down and did, and I hit him with three more
left hooks an' I had the guy in trouble.

Y'know, as many years as I've been brawlin', ya
still never know 'bout what's goin' on deep inside
a man. When ya think he's goin' down, when ya
think he's about to say the pain ain't worth the
profit, all of a sudden somethin' inside rings a bell,
lights a fire, and that man explodes with pride!
And they fight back harder when they're hurt than
when they ain't. And that's what Creed done. All
of a sudden he drilled me with a left-right combination in the face an' hooked twice. He started
yellin' at me about how I'm gonna go down, and
how his sister hits harder than me, and how he's
just playin' with me, because he's gonna destroy
me this round. I jabbed at Creed three times, and
believe it or not, every one of them tagged him. I
think I was startin' to get the range. Creed was
backpeddlin', and he hit me with three lefts, a
right, an' another left. My strategy just went out
the window—now it was, what ya call in ring talk,
a pier-six brawl. I lowered my head like you see

football players do an' I charged Creed. I rammed
him against the chest an' pinned him against the
turnbuckle. I bit down hard on the mouthpiece. I
do that when I throw my hardest shots. I whipped
two left hooks to the champ's head, then a right,
an' another left to the body. Creed tried to slide
along the ropes, an' I done somethin' I never been
able to do. I shadowed him, step for step! I nailed
him with three more lefts that drove him the other
way. He tried to turn me into the ropes, but I
hooked him with my arm around the waist an'
flung him back into the corner. I was feelin'
stronger than I ever felt in my life. Creed clinched
and spun me into the corner an' then cut loose
with a couple combinations an' hooks of his own. I
knew it had to end. I ducked the last hooks an'
threw a right to the body, an' Creed threw a right
to my head. I threw another left-right to the body
an' I seen somethin' red come out around the
bottom of Creed's eye.

The champ was cut!

I had the feelin' we was even now.

I said the next five rounds belonged all to the
champion. And he deserved 'em. He was really
makin' a big mess outta my face. Much better than
he done the first time. But I was relaxin'. I know
that sounds kinda stupid, but I was relaxin'. I was
takin' the beatin', but I was calmin' down. I
was doin' somethin' new.

I was thinkin'.

I was usin' my brain insteada just my body. I
was plannin'. I was plannin' ahead what I was gonna
do in maybe two rounds. I was slippin' into kind
of a fog. Y'know, it's that feelin' ya get when ya
go to sleep, an' sometimes ya think the bed is
floatin' an' turnin' an' everythin' sounds far away.

Maybe that's what dying people feel like. I ain't sure.

But I didn't just want to go the distance no more, I wanted to win, an' I didn't want to win just for myself. I wanted to win for the people around me. An' they was givin' me their best. I felt the crowd pushin' me harder an' harder an' harder; then I didn't hear the crowd no more. All I could hear was my heartbeat an' the wind being sucked through my mouthpiece.

And them punches. They was somethin' to see. Creed's red glove was comin' right into my face like some sorta animal. It just rammed in there. And the more I got hit, the slower everythin' was. That happens sometimes. When ya fight a lot, everythin' slows down. It's like fighters have this empty room, y'know, deep inside, an' the more pain, an' the more ya get nailed, an' the more tired ya are, the deeper ya go into this here room y'have. And it's kind of a private room where there's nothin'. Nothin'. There's no light bulbs, no music, nothin' —it's just you. And if ya really wanna win bad enough, ya gotta fight ya' way outta that dark room, back up them stairs, until ya come back to the real world an' battle hard! A coupla times I been knocked down in that room an' I stayed there, but I wasn't goin' to occupy it tonight. An' I knew Creed was feelin' the same thing.

Y'know, we weren't fightin' for no money or for no cheers or for no newspapers; it was for somethin' else that I don't know, it's almost religious. There's no reason, an' I don't even really understand why, but ya just do it an' ya never ask no questions why ya do it. Ya go with that flow. A couple of times I felt myself thinkin' in my head about death an' angels and things that ya don't see on the corner,

an' that scared me. An' I don't know what brought
that on; maybe I was more hurt than I figured, an'
every time I got scared I started punchin' harder. I
sure didn't want to die in the ring. Yeah, there was
maybe twenty-five thousand people around, an' it
would be what you call a well-attended funeral.

Y'know, fightin' ain't right. I only wish I knew
why God made me be a fighter. It made no sense.
Y'could never get ahead doin' it. Every punch I
knew weren't makin' me any smarter. I knew I
was maybe becomin' really damaged. And a coupla
years later I'd end up in some hospital outside
Trenton, New Jersey, talkin' to other guys who made
no sense either, an' that was scary.

Creed just hit me with a tremendous hook, and I
swayed sideways across the ring an' the ropes burned
into my back.

I'm glad that happened! I almost forgot what
kind of fight I was in.

My arms was heavy and they felt like they had
grown a foot. I threw a tired left hook and crouched
very low. Creed was tired, too, and he threw a slow
but strong left uppercut an' left hook, and another
right uppercut, an' this here left hook. Creed's jab
was pretty well gone. I had been poundin' his
shoulder every chance I got. When I couldn't reach
the jaw, I hit him on the shoulder—so all Creed had
now was a very good right hand. He never would
lose that right. When the right was gone, so was he.
An' I was still thinkin' about that right hand just as
he let it fly. I felt like he tore half my face off. I
was hurt this time, an' I could feel the blood just
pumpin' through my skin an' down my face. Creed
threw another right. Bang, right on the chin! He
was smokin' an' connected with a left hook. Bang!
An' another straight right, a left-right combination,

an' what I think was three more rights. I say I think, 'cause I couldn't see outta the right side of my face any more. This was it. No backin' off.

I went like an animal, an' I grabbed him around the waist an' pushed him into the corner an' unloaded with everythin' I had—hook, hook, hook, hook, an' three rights. Creed was in what ya call a frenzy. If we was real animals, we woulda spit the mouthpieces out an' tried to rip each other's throat.

I heard the best sound I had heard in what felt like hours, y'know—the bell. The referee jumped in between us an' we staggered into our corners. I shook my head at the referee, so he knew that I was feelin' fine. That was the biggest lie I ever told in my life. But I did somethin' I never thought I would ever do, an' it's funny, 'cause Creed done the same thing. We turned back, touched gloves, then went back to our corners to try to get some healin'. I sat down an' Mickey leaned his face close. "How's the eye?"

". . . it works," I said and gulped air.

In his corner the champ was breathing painfully, and his face was almost as badly swollen as his opponent's. The man seemed driven by only one objective. To knock out the challenger. Not to win on points, like last time. Not to be satisfied with thoroughly outboxing and maneuvering the man, but simply to destroy him. To send him into a world of unconsciousness.

"He's going—he's going!" the champ said, almost to himself.

"You got him on points," his trainer said, and applied a coagulant to a cut above the champ's eye. "Forget the knockout! Just stick and move. Three more minutes! This man's breakin' you up inside! Stay away!"

"It ain't going to be like last time—I gotta drop him!"

I was startin' to feel a little bit better. It's amazin' how much of his strength a fighter can get back in sixty seconds. And I knew I only had three more minutes to do that, which kinda helped my morale, you might say. I was thinkin' about how I was goin' to fight this last round, an' I had my battle plan almost worked out when I heard Mickey's voice smash into my ear. "You can't do this no more!"

"I know what I'm doin'!" I said an' I was 'bout to say some more when the referee come over.

"Rock, if you get in trouble again, I gonna stop it!" he said and walked away.

I yelled at him, "Please, don't stop nothin'!"

"Call it off—you can't win unless ya knock him out! You're gettin' killed out there!" Mickey screamed.

"It's my life!"

"He's gonna kill you—you wanna go blind?! This is it! This is our last chance! You gotta switch now!"

"No tricks. I think I can win—I don't need no tricks, Mick!"

"You crazy?! He's ready to drop you. Switch now, he's ready!"

"No tricks, I don't need no tricks!" I said and stood up.

"Then go to the body! Break his ribs. Don't let him breathe, Rock!"

As the bell rang, the commentators leaned closer to the monitors and watched the fighters approach the center of the ring with anticipation. "Here we are in the fifteenth round, and in my opinion, this has got to be even more grueling than the first fight. Why they haven't stopped it, God only knows," Bill Baldwin said.

"I have Apollo well ahead—all he has to do is stay away and he'll retain his title—but he's in there with a hellcat from Philly who's not about to lie down!"

I seen Apollo come out, take a deep breath, an' start to circle to the left. He flicked three jabs and then two hard rights into my face. Creed switched directions and threw two more jabs, a right and a left, then missed!

Christmas mornin', y'know what I mean!

I jumped forward an' put all my weight behind a left hook that nearly knocked Creed off his feet. I seen his eyes glass over right away, and I knew he was shook bad. He tried to backpedal, but I caught him with three more left hooks, then a right, then another left; then, for the first time, Creed almost went down.

"It's incredible! Balboa has nearly floored the champ! A leaping hook caught the exhausted champion off guard! Creed doesn't know where he is; he's fighting on blind instinct. Balboa is staggering from exhaustion—now it's all conditioning and guts!" screamed the commentators.

"Show him who you are! Show him your fire! Hook, hook, hook!" Mickey bellowed.

"I can't believe it! Apollo must be out on his feet—but he's challenging Balboa to come ahead!" one commentator yelled.

I could hear the Spectrum almost splittin' with noise, an' I wanted to do somethin' really great an' steamed ahead an' tried to blast Creed with a left hook to the body, an' it connected, 'cause the champ fell against the ropes. I started to move in, when

Creed leaned back against the ropes an' greeted me with a stiff right hand an' moved to the center of the ring. Oh, no! It looked like Creed got a second wind, 'cause then he hit me with punch after punch after punch, an' I felt myself givin' way. The legs was startin' to buckle, an' I was goin' back into that dark room where everythin' is quiet.

"I can't believe it—Balboa was caught by ripping combinations, and now he's in trouble!"

"He's going down—Creed's punches are landing at will—how much can he take?!"

"What's keeping him up? Creed is definitely trying for the knockout, but the southpaw is taking the champion's best!"

I kept stumblin', an' Creed hit me with another combination, an' another, an' I felt myself buckle in half. Three more uppercuts an' my hands were hangin' down at my waist, an' there was nothin' I could do to keep 'em up. My face was bein' hit again, an' again, an' again. It didn't hurt no more 'cause everythin' was numb—I just wanted to keep movin' ahead. I had to take his best. I threw a left an' Creed threw a right, and I threw a right hook and Creed countered with his right. Somehow I got under his jab and drove a right hook and a left hook to Creed's jaw, an' the champion went back on the ropes again.

I spit out my mouthpiece 'cause I needed more air, an' Creed hit me three times, but they was weak. This was it; I had 'bout fifteen seconds more fightin' left in me, an' after that I was just gonna be an unconscious pile of meat lyin' on the floor.

I tagged him with three left-right combinations an' kept hookin' and hookin', hopin' them hooks was strikin' home, 'cause I couldn't see no more. Damn! Creed again come back with his own flurry, an' I felt myself fallin' back. Now it was toe-to-toe all the way. He hit me to the head an' I hit him to the body. He nailed me with another combination, but I snuck in three more left hooks to the body, an' I think the last hook really took the wind out of him, 'cause he bent over backwards an' was almost pawin' at me like he was sayin', Go away.

This was my time! After this, no more chances!

I went underneath his right hand an' dug hook after hook after hook into his ribs. Creed was just standin' there in front of me, lookin' like he was in another world. I felt almost sorry, 'cause there was somethin' in his eyes that showed like he was a little boy sayin', Let's not fight no more, this is stupid. He was right, but I couldn't stop now. I hit him with a left hook an' he went back a step. I hit him with another left hook, an' my lungs were ready to blow up.

God, could he take it! He's great!

I pulled my left hand back as far as I could and swung with everythin' I had left. It landed on the champ's chin. My hand felt like I just hit a concrete door, an' the next thing I knew, we were floatin'. It was like I was floatin' an' dreamin'. I never felt nothin' like it. It was almost peaceful. I could see out of the corner of my eye that Creed was floatin' with me. All this floatin' an' peace crashed against the side of my head when I found myself layin' face-down on the canvas. I couldn't believe it! I thought the fight was over an' I was home in bed. Now everythin' was comin' back to me. I looked over an' seen Creed was layin' next to me, an' I heard the crowd screamin' about getting up, get on your feet! I seen the timekeeper poundin' his hand on the canvas . . . two, three! I reached for the rope an' tried to drag myself to my feet. I was tryin' to figure out

what had happened. All I knew now was me an'
Creed was in a race to get on our feet. I reached for
the second rope, but slipped down again. I got
scared an' reached back up even harder this time.

". . . five, six!" the referee said.

The commentators appeared to be on the brink
of insanity, screaming into the microphones. "Un-
believable! Both men are down! Exhausted! Beaten!
Both are being counted out—Creed and Balboa are
both trying to beat the count! In this case, if Creed
gets up he'll retain his title!"

"If Balboa makes it, he'll be the new world
heavyweight champion—Balboa's on one knee!"

At Rocky's house, Adrian and Paulie were on
their feet, inches from the television screen. Paulie
shook his fist at the tube and bellowed, "Get up,
Rock—get up, Rocky! Get up!"

"Please get up!" Adrian cried.

I seen Creed move to the second rope; we were
both about even.

"Seven!

"Eight!"

Through all them people I could hear Mickey's
voice knifin' through the noise. "Come on, show
your heart! Come on, do it! Show your heart!"
Mickey screamed.

Everythin' looked like it was under water. I heard
the referee say "Nine!" and it sounded like it was
comin' from the back of a tunnel. This *was* it. No
more after this; this is what you call the end of the
line. I bit down as hard as I could on my mouthpiece, gripped, leaped for the top rope, grabbed it,
an' pulled myself up.

"Ten!"

The crowd screamed louder than I had ever heard anythin' scream, an' the referee come over and grabbed my hand, but I was fallin' again. I fell into Mickey's arms an' he pulled me back to the corner. I looked back at Apollo and felt bad seein' him hangin' on to the second rope, still on one knee. A great guy.

I started to cry. I didn't cry 'cause I was hurt or tired or sad. I cried 'cause the contest was over. Not the whole contest of boxin', but the contest of me chasin' this thing for years an' years an' years.

The pain.

The blood.

The fear.

It was over.

I laid my head on Mickey's shoulder an' cried.

". . . I think you got potential, kid," Mickey said and held me close to him.

"He did it!" Baldwin chortled into the microphones. "At the very last second, Balboa got to his feet—he made it! Rocky Balboa has just shocked the entire sporting world as it has never before been shocked! He is now crying from fatigue and the excitement!"

Paulie hugged Adrian, and they stared at the bedlam on the television screen. "He's the best!"

"Yes . . ." Adrian said, and cried.

I started to get my legs back and stood up straight and seen what was goin' on with Apollo. As much as Apollo had always been takin' shots at me, I still liked the guy. The man was a tower of power.

A tower of pride.

I knew tonight was killin' him inside. I waited for the ring announcer to finish talkin'. ". . . in a stunning upset, the new heavyweight champion of the world, Rocky Balboa!" The Philly people went crazy again, an' I waved an' passed all them reporters, an' finally I got to Apollo's corner. He was crying, too. I patted him on the shoulder, and he turned around and looked at me for a second. "You're great . . ." I said. ". . . good luck." Me and Apollo kind of embraced, and he did somethin' that I'll never forget as long as I live. Apollo raised my hand to the crowd an' draped his heavyweight championship belt over my shoulder. I wanted to say thanks as soon as he did that thing with the belt, but he started to move out of the ring and back into his life again.

These guys with headphones started to push the guys with the cameras away and tried to get me in front of this television camera.

"Rocky, how do you feel?"

"I didn't think I was going to make it—he's great!"

"As heavyweight champion, what are your plans now?"

"I'm goin' home! Can I have a microphone?"

"Give the champ the microphone! Give him the mike!" one of the commentators screamed.

They lowered this microphone from a cord that come out of the top of the ceiling there and held it in front of my face, and I tried to catch my breath to talk. "Excuse me—excuse me—I can't believe it —I can't believe it! I want to thank Apollo Creed for fightin' me an' thank Mickey for trainin' me, and I want to thank God for helpin' me—an' except for my kid bein' born, this is the best night in the history of my life! ! !"

I wiped this sweat away that was runnin' into my

eyes an' I heard somebody in the crowd scream, "We love you, Rock."

"I love you, too! An' I just want to say somethin' to my wife . . ." I looked around to where the camera was, an' I raised this beautiful gold championship belt above my head an' yelled as loud as I would ever yell in my whole life. "Yo, Adrian, I did it!!!"